I0619425

BENEFIT
of the
DOUBT

MONTANA PERIL ~ BOOK 1

by Lesley Ann McDaniel

ISLANDS OF INTRIGUE: SAN JUANS series

Christian Romantic Suspense

The Unrelenting Tide – by Lynnette Bonner
Book 1

Tide Will Tell – by Lesley Ann McDaniel
Book 2

MONTANA HEARTS series

(Heartsong Presents)
Christian Romance

Lights, Cowboy, Action
Book 1

Big Sky Bachelor
Book 2

Rocky Mountain Romance
Book 3

Chapter 1

In the shadowy walkway outside her motel room, Carrie Yost fumbled with the key. Her hands shook as she jabbed it into the keyhole, then jimmied the knob until it turned and the door groaned open. She slipped inside, shoved the door shut, and twisted the deadbolt, then gave the knob a tug to confirm its security.

As she leaned her back against the door, the breakneck pace of her heart alarmed her. Drawing in a deep breath, she willed her adrenaline to dissipate so she'd be able to sleep. All she needed were a couple of good hours.

Pushing her weight from the door, she strained to see in the bit of light easing around the edges of the curtained window next to her. This looked like a standard motel room with a double bed, nightstand, TV. The cracked-open bathroom door on the far wall taunted her with the ominous darkness it mostly concealed. Shouldn't motel maids be required to leave the light on for late-night arrivals? Or would the implication that someone had recently been in the room, and might still be there, serve as more of a threat than a comfort?

Slowly, she edged through the room, not sure if turning on a lamp would make her feel safe or exposed. How *could* she know when she'd never been in this kind of situation before?

Right now, she just wanted to make sure the room was clear of any threats, then fall into an unconscious heap on the bed long enough to restore her energy for the next leg of her journey.

But where was that journey going to take her? And how was she supposed to figure that out, since she didn't even know why she was running?

Creeping closer to the bathroom, she lifted her hand, then gave the door a swift shove as though to warn anyone who might be standing on the other side that she was onto them. Like her mere presence would intimidate the kind of person who would want someone dead badly enough to foresee their checking in to a particular room in a middle-of-nowhere motel, then hide there, waiting for them.

When nothing happened, she reached through the doorway and flicked on the light, then peered inside. Empty. She quickly checked the small frosted-glass window over the tub, then shut off the light and went back out to the main room.

Weary from a lack of sleep and her overtaxed nervous system, she plunked down on the bed. Yes, she needed to rest, but she should check on Lucas first. The question was . . . how could she get ahold of him when *she* had his phone?

Maybe if she scrolled through the contacts on her own phone, she'd find a mutual friend. Someone she could trust to at least go check on him. She reached into her purse, which was secured over her shoulder, then felt around, her adrenaline spiking again. Where was her phone?

Oh, no. She'd been using the GPS in the car and she'd left it on the console. Why hadn't she been thinking?

A high-speed debate rattled her tired brain. She could just leave it out there. No, she needed the security of having it with her. And what if Lucas called? She had to be there for him. There was no choice but to go back out into the inky black night and retrieve it.

It would be okay. She'd move quickly. No one had followed her; she'd been certain of that. Considering that she'd spent the last few hours driving along this mostly-unlit stretch of isolated highway somewhere in Montana, there was no way anyone could have tailed her undetected.

She unlocked the door, then slipped back out onto the dim walkway and pulled the door shut. She hesitated. If she left it unlocked, that would make for a quicker re-entry, but . . . she looked over at the other wing of the L-shaped building that sat parallel to the highway and thought about her car, parked behind that part of the building.

It had made so much sense fifteen minutes ago, when she'd pulled off the road and made sure she hadn't been followed. If someone was on her trail, they might slow down to check for her car in the lot, but they would keep going if they didn't see it. That was probably something she'd read in a book or seen in a movie, since her actual life had afforded her zero training for this kind of thing.

It would be impossible to keep an eye on her room once she rounded that dark corner. She gave the knob an extra tug to ensure that it had locked.

Looking around, she saw nothing but a few cars parked next to the building, a sliver of moon, and the buzzing neon sign proclaiming that the Big Sky Motor Inn still had vacancies. She wrapped her arms around herself—grateful for the warmth of her sweater, but wishing she had grabbed a jacket before she'd taken off—and cut across the quiet parking lot.

In spite of her attempt at stealth movements, her loafers made a crunching sound in the gravel that seemed loud enough to wake the dead. Glancing over her shoulder, she hurried her steps. This place was probably quaint in the light of day, but right now it felt like the perfect setting for a slasher movie. That thought sent a chill through her that propelled her to hasten her steps even more.

Once at her car, she retrieved the phone, then darted back to the room and scooted inside.

Again, she shut the door behind herself and locked it. Stepping forward, she brought up her contact list and started scrolling. How was it that she knew so many people, but still had no one to turn to in a crisis?

Groaning, she moved around to the far side of the bed. There had to be someone—

From out of nowhere, a powerful arm encircled her waist, yanking her backward. Then a gloved hand clamped over her mouth, blocking her scream.

Clawing desperately at the hand, she fought for air. A smell, spicy and somehow familiar, thickened in her nostrils.

Cloves.

Her assailant snapped her phone from her hand and flung her onto the bed. Rolling to her back, she flailed for anything she could use as a defense. She hurled the bedside lamp at the hulking dark form that hovered over her. He dodged as the lamp barely grazed him. In the next horrifying seconds, he lunged, grabbed a pillow from the bed, and pressed it over her face.

He's going to kill me.

Then another thought struck her. Gulping for air, she found her purse still strapped to her side. Somehow, she managed to yank it open and shove her hand into it.

Please. Please!

There it was! Her keyring. And the pocketknife she kept on it.

Fighting lightheadedness, she used both hands to flick the knife open.

With a burst of strength and determination, she drew up the knife and thrust it at her attacker. He let out a guttural wail and released his grip on the pillow. She pushed it from her face, wheezing in air.

As the featureless form stumbled back, she caught sight of him clutching at the knife in his throat. She watched only long enough to see him crumple into a heap on the floor.

In a blurry panic, she somehow made it out the door and sprinted full force toward her car. All she could think was that she had just stabbed a man and he might be dead.

She had to get away. *Now.*

But moments later, as she slammed to a stop against the driver's side door, a horrible realization hit. Her key fob was on the ring with the knife. *What now?*

She darted back to the corner of the building and peeked around at the office, but it was dark. Briefly, she considered going back to the room, but what if the man was still alive? What if he was dead? Which thought terrified her more? No, all she could do now was run.

Run for her life.

She took off in what she thought was the direction of the road.

Then a sound broke through the silence. She glanced up just as a pair of headlights appeared in the distance. Someone who could help her?

As she charged toward the vehicle, its outline grew clearer. Some kind of truck hauling a trailer. Waving her arms, she ran till her feet hit pavement.

It roared past.

Then, the brakes screeched and the truck pulled to the shoulder. *Hallelujah.*

Again, she ran toward it, vaguely aware of a man getting out and rushing toward her.

"I . . . I . . ." she stammered, short on breath.

"Come on." He grabbed her arm and tugged her safely to the side of the road. "What's wrong?"

"I . . . just . . ." She fought to get the words out. ". . . killed someone."

Lesley Ann McDaniel

Chapter 2

Am I crazy?

Carrie seriously questioned her sanity as she trudged back toward the motel, with a careful eye on the stranger who kept pace several feet away. Even if she wasn't actually certifiable, she sure must *look* like an escapee from someplace with either "sanitarium" or "asylum" in the name. Charging at an oncoming vehicle to get the driver's attention. Now returning to the scene of her possible crime with that driver—an absolute stranger.

Yes. Crazy.

But it had made sense to her rattled mind that a truck towing some kind of trailer and coming from the opposite direction of her own initial approach to the motel wouldn't be driven by someone who gunning for her. And, like it or not, she needed help.

The truck driver, who—judging from his work shirt, Levi's, and cowboy hat—must be some kind of rancher or something, had calmly listened to her babbling, then insisted on accompanying her back to the motel to piece together what had happened. Now, as they approached the room, she held back a few steps in case she might have to run again.

"It's that one there." Her raised hand shook so badly she could barely point.

He looked to her for confirmation, then reached for the door. With a light shove, it opened to the dark room. He flicked on the light.

Carrie flinched, then stared incredulously as he entered ahead of her. What was going on?

No body.

No blood.

The bedside lamp, which she could have sworn she'd hurled at her attacker, stood in its proper position on the nightstand. The bedding wasn't even rumpled.

The faint smell of cloves still hung in the air. But as quickly as she thought she'd detected it, it was gone. Had she imagined that too?

"You sure this is the right room?"

"Uh . . ." Jerking out of her stupor, she checked the number on the door. "Y . . . yes. I . . . don't understand."

The truck driver . . . rancher . . . good Samaritan, looked at her from where he'd stopped on the far side of the bed. Right about where the dead body was supposed to be. He made a visual sweep of the space then let his studied gaze linger on her. As she met his wary eyes, her breath caught. Now that she could see him in decent lighting, her heart made a funny little skip-beat.

Dark hair. Chiseled features. Rugged good looks under that hint of stubble.

Oh my . . .

She forced her focus off of him. This was no time to get distracted from the very serious issue at hand.

"So . . ." His eyes—deep brown and undeniably compassionate, if she wasn't mistaken—scanned the room again. "Who was this person?"

How could she possibly answer that, since she had no idea? And the little she did know only made the situation more puzzling. She wasn't about to spill her story to someone she hadn't even really met—heart-stoppingly handsome or not. Maybe if she diverted his attention, he wouldn't notice that she hadn't answered the question.

"I had only just walked into the room. I was standing here when he grabbed me from behind." She moved into the position where she'd been when the attack happened. "I was here, checking my phone and . . ." Her voice trailed off as her little re-enactment jarred her memory. Her phone. Where was it?

"So he came from in there." He crossed to the bathroom and turned on the light, then gave that space a quick check. "Nothing out of the ordinary now."

She looked around. Lifted the pillows. Checked under the bed. No phone.

"What's wrong?" He took a few steps closer to her, keeping a respectful distance.

"It's just that, I thought I dropped my phone when he grabbed me, but I don't see it anywhere."

She felt for her purse which, remarkably, remained draped across her body. She gave it a cursory check, knowing she wouldn't find her phone. "It's not there."

"Those your keys?" As he moved around her to get to the table that held the TV and another lamp, she glanced over at her keyring. The one with the pocketknife on it.

"Yeah." The shaking in her hands that had eased slightly returned as she reached for the keys. Reluctantly, she opened the knife. The blade looked clean. Like it had never been used. How was that possible?

Had she just imagined the whole incident?

"I . . . thought I . . . used this on him . . ."

"You mean, you stabbed him?"

"I . . . don't know . . ."

"Uh-huh." He eyed her like he'd probably just decided she was a lunatic. "Well . . ." Making a final survey of the room, he rubbed the back of his neck. "We'll have to call the sheriff."

Her stomach sank. Everything in her screamed *run!* Why had she put her trust in this stranger?

"No." The woman's eyes widened as she shook her head and held up a hand like a shield. "No sheriff."

Joe stopped rubbing his neck and gave her another once-over. In spite of the section of blond hair that stuck out in the wrong direction, the curls draping her shoulders looked soft to the touch. Makeup that had probably been meant to enhance her pretty blue eyes now made her look a little like a football player. He couldn't help but notice that behind her dazed look, she was exceptionally beautiful.

And scared. What had really happened to her?

Not wanting to spook her any further, he held up both hands in what he hoped she'd see as a calming gesture.

"Okay. No sheriff." All traces of drowsiness had vanished from Joe's body, and his mind had clicked into high alert. The way his heart raced, he might not ever sleep again. "You want to tell me why?"

Her eyes darted around the room, like the answer might be written on a cue card somewhere. "I can't really explain it. I just think it might make things worse."

"All right, then." He nodded slowly. "Tell me what you want to do instead."

"I think the best thing would be for me to just leave. I can drive until it gets light out, then figure out what I need to do."

"I might be out of line saying this, but you seem a little . . ." He searched for the right word. ". . . worked up. You think you're fit to drive?"

"I'm fine." Gripping her keys, she angled toward the door.

"Wait. Don't you have a bag, or something?"

"No." She tapped her purse. "Just this."

"Uh-huh." As weird as that seemed, it somehow fit with the rest of this scenario. "Why don't I see you to your car."

A slight shake of her head. She paused for a moment, then nodded. "Fine. Thanks."

They stepped back out into the night that seemed to have gotten brisker in the few minutes they'd spent inside. An owl hooted, and she nearly jumped out of her skin.

He trailed along next to her, keeping a good distance between them so as not to further alarm her. The thought of leaving this poor woman to her own devices seemed . . . what? Unchristian? Or at the very least, unchivalrous. Grandma had raised him better than to abandon a woman when she clearly needed help. Glancing skyward, he shot up a quick prayer. *What would You have me do here?*

An idea settled in his gut, sending it into an unpleasant churn.

"You know—" He cleared his throat. "—there's not much of a moon tonight. I'm heading as far as Rockford. You can trail behind my rig if you want. That way, the road ahead of you won't be so dark and hard to see."

"Rockford." Brow furrowing, she shot him a glance. "That's how far?"

He shrugged. "About another seventy miles or so. I own a ranch just outside of town."

She pushed a strand of hair behind her ear and nodded again, saying nothing.

When they passed the last car in the lot, he frowned. "Uh . . . where did you say you parked?"

"I didn't say. I'm just around here. In the back."

Behind the building? Whatever was going on with this woman, it just kept getting stranger. He followed her around to the back of the motel where, sure enough, a sedan sat in the darkness.

He squinted. A Lexus. Fancier than he was used to seeing around here.

A quick look at her plate told him she was from Washington, and he made a mental note of the number. Couldn't hurt to call Jeremy in the morning and have him check on her welfare.

"Um . . . thanks." Looking like she might want to add something more, she opened the driver's side door.

"Yeah. I can go ahead and just—" He angled his head in the direction of the highway, where he'd left his rig. "—wait till I see that you're behind me before I take off."

She nodded, hesitating before pulling her gaze from his.

When she finally did, he took a step, then stopped. Something about her car caught his eye and he bent down to get a better look.

"Hang on." Recalling that he had a flashlight app on his phone, he took it from his pocket as he knelt next to her front tire.

"What is it?" Her voice came out sounding even more pinched as she leaned toward him.

"Looks like someone wants you to stay put." He looked up at her. "Your tire's been slashed."

Chapter 3

Carrie sat in the passenger seat of the rancher's truck, staring straight ahead at the seemingly endless stretch of dark highway. She felt so bone-weary, her eyes barely stayed open. But sleep would be out of the question.

Wetting her lips, she realized that her mouth felt as dry as dust. Funny, she hadn't even thought about stopping for food or water in all the time she'd been on the road. There was nothing like the fear of death to kill a person's appetite.

"Hungry?"

A chill passed through her at the implication that he'd read her thoughts. "I'm fine."

"You sure? I might have some jerky in the—"

"No. Thank you." *I'm vegan* trailed silently after, seeming too personal a detail to share.

In spite of the heater that he'd thoughtfully cranked up, her hands wouldn't stop shaking. Had she only imagined the attack? Could extreme fatigue, hunger, and adrenal overload make a person delusional? Probably, but how would that explain the slash in her tire? That couldn't be a coincidence.

What was she going to do? Whoever had sabotaged her car had no doubt been hanging out nearby. Lurking in the darkness in anticipation of her coming back out alone.

Stranded. Vulnerable.

Thank goodness she'd accepted her Samaritan's offer of an escort. His presence had no doubt made the difference between life and—

"There's coffee in that thermos." He jabbed a thumb toward the floor at her feet. "If you'd like some."

She shook her head. Accepting coffee—a symbol of comfort— from this admittedly kind man struck her as simultaneously appealing and unnerving. "Thanks, anyway."

She lowered the visor and flipped open the little mirror, hoping to see if any headlights trailed behind them. But she couldn't see past the livestock trailer they had in tow. That thing was enormous. Leave it to her to hitch a ride in the most conspicuous vehicle on the planet.

Good going, Carrie.

"I . . . uh . . . have a little first aid kit in the glove box. You might want to have a look at that cut on your face."

What?

She checked the mirror again. Sure enough, her cheek was bleeding. When had that happened? She must have done it to herself when she tried to pry the man's hand from her mouth.

"Thanks." She easily found the small plastic box containing the basics of first aid. Tearing open an alcohol wipe, she wondered what this guy must be thinking.

"Name's Joe. Joe Moder."

His rich, warm voice cut into her thoughts, and she jerked like a spooked animal. She almost laughed at the thought that he might be speaking in the same voice he used to soothe his horses. Or cows. Or ... whatever that was back there.

He paused, probably hoping she'd reflexively offer her own name in response. When she didn't, he went on. "My ranch is just this side of Rockford. I can take you into town if you want ..."

He let the sentence trail off, like she might pick it up by filling in the blanks of her intended plan. Which so far, didn't exactly exist.

"Sounds good. Thanks." Even as she said it, her mind raced. Rockford sounded vaguely familiar, like it was one of the blink-and-you'll-miss-it towns she'd passed through before stopping at the motel. Would anything be open? An all-night diner, maybe?

"Course, nothing'll be open in town for a few hours yet." He went on, again providing the eerie suggestion of clairvoyance. "You got anyone you can call?"

Her lack of an immediate answer seemed suspicious; she knew. But she couldn't exactly admit that she had no idea who to trust right now. Besides, any information she offered would only stir up more questions. "I'll figure something out."

"Yeah." He cast her a quick sideways glance. "I'm sure you will."

The silence echoed with so many unasked questions, she wanted to scream just to break it. What had she been thinking, leaving her car behind? It wasn't like she had money for a rental. Not that a town like Rockford would be likely to support a Hertz franchise, but still.

Of course, she had money in her bank account, along with her emergency credit card. But both of those options seemed risky. She had no way of knowing what she was up against. If there might be even the remotest chance that she could be tracked down—

". . . she has arthritis. Rheumatoid."

The awareness that Joe had been making small talk to fill the silence startled her from her fretting.

"She's stubborn, that's for sure. But she means everything to me. That's why I'm on the road so late. A man with an ounce of sense would have stopped for the night."

"I . . ." She floundered with her thoughts. "I'm glad you didn't."

"Didn't what?" An eyebrow shot up along with one side of his mouth. "Have any sense?"

"No." An actual chuckle huffed out. "I'm glad you didn't stop for the night." Small talk felt good. Normal. "But I'm sorry about your . . ." Who was the woman he'd been telling her about? His wife?

Probably not, if she had severe arthritis. But there no doubt *was* a wife in the picture, considering that this guy had to be somewhere in the neighborhood of thirty, and a major catch, to say the very least. "I'm sorry."

A quick glance at his hands on the wheel gave her no clue. From this angle and in this light, she couldn't tell if he wore a ring or not.

"Thanks." Emotion seemed to catch in his throat. He cleared it, then went on. "You got family?"

He had offered up that question like polite conversation, but she knew he was fishing. Who wouldn't, considering the circumstances?

"Um . . . not really." Not exactly a lie. She hadn't said no.

Several more seconds of silence ticked by. Then he let out something between a sigh and a groan and pinched the bridge of his nose. His right hand came up between them like a signal that he wanted to stop their little game of interrogation-avoidance.

"Look. I know this might sound strange, but I wouldn't feel right just dropping you off, even if something *was* open at this hour. You're obviously in some kind of a bind and you need sleep so you can think straight."

All true. But this was *her* problem, not his. "I don't—"

"Hear me out. We have plenty of room at the house, and you're more than welcome to stay the night. Or what's left of it. Then, come morning, I can drive you into town. Deal?"

A rush of ragged-edged emotions washed through her. A good solid sleep sounded better than anything, and the thought of an actual bed—maybe even some food—overpowered her thinking.

Before she could talk herself out of it, she squeaked out a feeble, "Okay."

He nodded. "Course, if we're going to be hosting you, it might be good to know your name."

Acid filled her throat. Visions of herself in one of those heroine-on-the-run movies, failing to respond to her made-up name, convinced her that she needed to soften his suspicion.

"Carrie." She coughed. "I'm Carrie."

He angled his head, probably waiting for her to add her last name. When she didn't, he nodded and let out a breath. "Pleasure to meet you, Carrie."

Her gaze lingered for a moment on his handsome face before she forced herself to look away. She was testing his patience. No doubt about it.

Chapter 4

Joe crossed around the front of the truck, rolling the kinks out of his shoulders—the result of both the long day of driving and the added stress of the night's events. Even more than usual, it felt good to be home.

Coming around to the passenger side, he glanced at the house. The lights glowed in practically every room downstairs. Which meant that Grandma, bless her soul, hadn't turned in yet.

His jaw clenched. He'd held out a vague hope that he wouldn't have to face her till he'd gotten a little sleep, but this was probably for the best. Better to talk to her now than to risk her running into their houseguest before he'd had time to explain why she was there.

Just as he reached for the passenger door, it eased open and Carrie swung her legs out of the cab. She gripped both sides of the doorframe, looking down as if she didn't quite trust that the ground would be there to catch her.

Joe instinctively reached out to help, but she shirked back. He retracted his hand. The woman was like a scared filly. What on God's green earth had happened to her?

After slowly easing herself out of the truck and shutting the door, she stood there with her arms wrapped around herself. She eyed the surrounding area like she might be worried about someone hiding in the barn or one of the other outbuildings.

"This is where you live?" Her tone held an edge of suspicion.

"Yep."

Thinking she'd follow, he started toward the house. But she just stood there, as if her feet had taken root.

He stopped. "You okay?"

"Sorry. Yes. It's just that . . ." Finally, she started moving. "I've never been to an actual ranch before. It's not quite what I expected."

"What did you expect?"

"I guess I don't really know." Her steps halted and she held a hand up toward the trailer. "Don't you have to unload your animals?"

"They'll be fine till morning." At her perplexed look, he added, "It's common practice, trust me. They'd rather not be disturbed till the sun comes up."

"Oh . . ." She started walking again, so slowly he half expected her to do an about face and say she'd rather sleep in the livestock trailer than take her chances in the house with him. Not that he blamed her. Now that he'd spent a little time with her, he could tell she wasn't some kind of thrill-seeker or risk-taker. Whatever had happened to her must have been pretty bad if her only option had been to accept a ride from a stranger.

He wanted to reassure her but, apart from *not* being a homicidal maniac, how was he supposed to do that?

They made their way in silence across the gravel drive, then up the walkway. He turned his focus upward as they approached the steps leading to the porch that spanned nearly the whole front of the house. "The place isn't normally lit up like a Christmas tree this time of the night."

"Oh?"

"Guess the welcoming committee's still awake."

She nodded, like his feeble attempt at humor had only made her more nervous—the opposite of what he'd been going for.

He chided himself as they climbed the steps. He always *had* been better at dealing with livestock than women. Which explained why he'd always had more success with ranching than romancing.

A sudden knot in his stomach vied with the pain in his shoulders for his attention. It hit him how this must look—creeping into the house at this hour of the night with a woman who looked like she'd been put through the wringer. Good thing they didn't have any close neighbors to witness their arrival.

And even once he explained to Grandma, that wouldn't be the end of it. Sure, she'd agree he'd done the right thing by not leaving Carrie stranded. But she might not agree with his decision to bring her—a total stranger—into their home. This was definitely a first for them.

A split second after he opened the front door, he knew that Grandma had spent her day making sure he wouldn't go to bed hungry. By the aroma that welcomed them, he'd bet a roast beef sandwich and a thick slice of apple pie waited for him in the kitchen. She knew him so well.

Taking a step back, he expected Carrie to enter, but she just stood there, staring wide-eyed into the foyer like she'd never seen how a front door worked.

"Something wrong?"

"It's just that ... you don't keep your door locked?"

"I lock up before I go to bed."

"But, your—"

"Joe ... ?"

The sound of Grandma's voice coming from inside seemed to catch Carrie off guard. She cast Joe a what-do-I-do look that he responded to with a sweeping gesture toward the entrance. Finally, she stepped inside.

He went in after her, then made a point of shutting and locking the door.

"Oh, honey, I was starting to get worried ..." Grandma stopped short in the doorway from the front room. She gazed quizzically at Carrie, then self-consciously tugged at the neckline of her robe. "Oh. You've brought a friend home."

Joe swallowed a nervous laugh. Those were the exact words she would have used back when he was a kid, walking in the door with a buddy from school or a stray dog. *Ah, simpler times.*

"Grandma. This is Carrie. She ran into some car trouble and she needs a place to stay the night."

He could feel his face reddening, as the appearance of the situation fully set in. This had to look bad to someone who didn't know the whole story. Of course, even *he* didn't know the whole story. Might not ever know it.

By the way one of Grandma's gray brows rose, he knew his red face hadn't gone unnoticed. But she chose to do the ladylike thing and ignore it.

"Carrie." Stepping forward, she held out both of her tiny hands to clasp one of Carrie's. "Welcome to our home."

"It's nice to meet you, Mrs. . . . ."

"Brannon. Joe's mother was my daughter, Mary."

Carrie seemed to relax just a bit. "It's nice to meet you, Mrs. Brannon."

"Are you hungry, dear?" Grandma asked, giving Carrie's hand an extra pat before taking a step toward the kitchen. "I could make you a sandwich, or—"

"No, thank you. I think I just need to sleep."

"I'll show you to the guest room, then. Joe, would you make me another cup of tea?"

Joe nodded, knowing full well it wasn't really a cup of tea that she wanted but the time it would take him to make it. This was her way of ensuring he didn't beat a hasty retreat to his own room before she had a chance to get the details out of him.

As Grandma led Carrie to the staircase, she tossed a look over her shoulder at him that said a hundred different things, none of which was, "I'm going to make this easy on you."

Letting out a long breath, he headed for the front room to retrieve her tea cup, then ambled on back to the kitchen. At least he had a minute to think through how much he wanted to reveal while Carrie was still under their roof. Lord knew, he didn't want to worry Grandma unnecessarily.

Stopping in the doorway, he chuckled. Sure enough, there on the table in the middle of the kitchen were a couple of plates. One held two thick slices of homemade bread with enough roast beef between them to feed two men. And on the other . . . he inhaled . . . apple pie. One thing was for sure, as long as he lived with Grandma, he never had to worry about getting too thin.

By the time she joined him at the table, the tea was half steeped and the sandwich half gone. She paused, pursed her lips, and lowered herself into the chair opposite him.

"So . . ." He swallowed a bite of sandwich and chased it with a swig of milk. "She tell you anything?"

"Only that her car broke down on the highway and you stopped to offer her a ride. That just didn't sound right."

"You don't think I'd stop for someone in trouble?"

"Of course. But you know how vulnerable a woman can feel in that kind of situation. You'd stop and call for a tow truck."

"Grandma, you know there's no cell service till you get closer to town. Besides, even if we'd had her car towed, she needed a place to bed down."

"Well, something's not right." Tugging at her robe, she shifted in the straight-back chair. "I just can't quite put my finger on what it is." She let out a *tsking* sound, absently bobbing her teabag up and down in the water. "Did you ask her where she's from? Where she was headed?"

"No, ma'am." Joe took another bite. "She seemed upset enough without me grilling her. I figured she'd talk if she felt more at ease."

Her eyes narrowed on him. "There's more, isn't there?"

He swallowed. "More?"

"Something you're not saying. I can tell."

Setting the remainder of his sandwich on his plate, Joe bowed to the inevitable. Grandma had a suspicion, and she wasn't going to rest—or let *him* rest—until he'd spilled everything he knew. Might as well not fight it. "You're right. There's more." He shoved his plate to the side and leaned forward. "I think she's in trouble."

"Oh . . .?" She mirrored his move. "What kind of trouble?"

"I don't know. Exactly." He took a deep breath and started in on the story.

When he got to the part about finding no one, living or dead, in the motel room, Grandma looked up from under her worry-creased brow. "My goodness."

"The thing is, there was no evidence of a struggle in that room. No blood. Nothing."

"Did you call Jeremy?"

"I wanted to. She said 'no sheriff.'"

"If someone attacked her, why wouldn't she want to involve the sheriff?"

"Beats me. Made me wonder . . ."

"You think she's not telling you the truth?"

"I don't know. She seemed pretty confused. Like maybe she didn't really *know* what had happened to her. And a woman traveling without a suitcase. Something's not right."

He went on, about the tire and their conversation in the truck, such as it was. "I asked if she had anyone she could call. She said no."

"No family?"

He shook his head. "But . . . I got the impression that might not be completely true. I don't know, Grandma . . ." Unable to resist the tempting aroma of cinnamon and butter, he picked up his fork and jabbed at the slice of pie. "Some guy hiding in her room . . . then an attack on her car. I think there's more to it than just a string of random bad luck."

She resolutely placed her hands in her lap. "I think she's running away from something."

"Yeah." He pointed his fork for emphasis. "The question is, is it something that got done to her or something she did."

"You think she might be running from the law?"

Savoring a bite of pie, he shrugged his eyebrows.

"Well." She pushed back from the table. "You'll call Jeremy in the morning." Picking up her still mostly full cup, she glanced up at the clock above the door. "Goodness, Joe. Keeping an old woman up until all hours of the night."

Smiling, he devoured the rest of his pie, then cleared his plates to the sink, where Grandma stood rinsing out her cup. He bent and kissed the side of her head. "Good night. And thanks for the snack."

"Hope it tides you over till breakfast." She patted his stomach. "Sleep well."

He paused a moment, watching as she headed toward the back bedroom, the one she had claimed after Grandpa had passed. She'd said it was because of its proximity to the kitchen, the room where she spent the majority of her time. But Joe knew it was because getting up and down those stairs had gotten painful.

A sigh slipped out. Probably not as painful as the lingering memories of Grandpa in the room upstairs. They still hadn't cleared out all of his things. Maybe one of these days.

He shook off that thought as he crossed to the back door and twisted the lock, recalling the look of alarm on Carrie's face as she'd gaped at the unlocked front door.

He shook that off too. Right now, all he wanted to think about was how good it would feel when his head hit the pillow.

Chapter 5

Carrie's eyes popped open and she sprang upright, her head feeling like a bowling ball that had just hit a strike. Next to her, a small gold clock told her it was a few minutes before eight. She hadn't meant to sleep so long. Everything in her world had been turned upside down and she needed to get on with setting it right.

Whatever that meant.

What day was this? She'd have to check in with work eventually. Of course, working independently bought her some time. It wasn't unusual for her to not show up or touch base for a few days.

The abrupt thought that she could vanish from the face of the earth and not be missed hit her like a brick. Normally, she liked that about her life. Or did she just tell herself that?

Drawing in a long breath, she blinked the grogginess from her eyes, then got a good look at the room she'd been too tired to pay much attention to the previous night. Tiny blue flowers on a white background covered the walls. Antique-looking furniture—a matching dresser and vanity, upholstered chair, and a bookcase filled with hardcovers—gave the appearance of having been there for several generations. She twisted to get a good look at the solid white metal bedframe. Simple, yet elegant. Under normal circumstances, this was a room she would have loved to linger in.

Sounds that were nothing like the city noise she was used to drew her attention to a large curtained window on the other side of the room. A rooster crowed. Birds sang. Somewhere off in the distance, a dog barked. It all seemed so peaceful.

Such a contrast to her reality.

Then the harshness of that reality hit like a bulldozer. Lucas was in trouble, and she had no idea why. Her gaze darted around the room. Where had she left her phone? What if he'd been trying to get ahold of her?

Then she remembered. She had no phone. It had been taken.

A sick feeling lurched at the memory of the attack. It seemed so hazy now, she could almost convince herself that she'd imagined it. If that man had been after her because of Lucas, why would he have taken her phone? Unless . . .

Of course. Lucas had given her *his* phone and had told her to keep it safe for him. The man must have thought that was what she had in her hand when he attacked her.

But why? What on earth could be so important that he would have killed her to get it?

Seeing her purse looped over the end of the footboard, she reached for it, then dug down to the inner pocket where she'd stashed her lunkheaded brother's phone. Maybe she could use it to somehow get through to him.

And figure out what was on it that was so all-fired important . . .

She pushed the button on the back, but nothing happened. Dead. *Great.* And of course, it required a different kind of charger than the one she kept in her car.

The car.

Her stomach buckled. Even if there was a shop in town that could sell her a new tire, did she have enough cash to pay for it?

She quickly counted out the bills in her wallet. Fifty-seven dollars. If she could get a deal, that might buy her a new tire. But would her insurance cover the cost of towing it all the way to Rockford? Did she dare use one of her cards and risk alerting whoever was after her of her whereabouts? A cold sweat broke out on her forehead. Time to get moving.

She pulled back the floral quilt she'd slept so peacefully under and groaned at the reminder that she was still dressed in the same outfit she'd put on for work the previous morning. Only now, it looked like it belonged in a rag bin. There wasn't much she could do about that.

She swung her feet from between the sheets, then jolted at the unexpected chill of the hardwood floor penetrating her thin trouser socks. As she stood, the sick feeling of knowing she'd been followed to the motel the night before seeped back into her belly. How could she be sure that the man she thought she'd stabbed hadn't seen her get into Joe's truck? Her gaze fixed on the window, and she inched toward it.

Taking care not to stand too close in case someone might be watching, she peered out through the opening in the lacy curtains. A deep blue sky shone through tree branches that swayed slightly, like they were dancing in a gentle morning breeze. Below her, Joe's truck sat in the gravel area next to the house, but the trailer was no longer attached to it. The small buildings and big white barn that had been dark and daunting last night looked downright charming in the light of day.

When she shifted to one side of the window, she could see the long gravel road they'd driven down the night before that had seemed miles long. It curved and disappeared over a rise, making it impossible to see the gate he'd gotten out to open several minutes before their arrival at the house.

There was no sign of anyone down there, which she found both alarming and reassuring. At least if someone had followed her from the motel, they would have a harder time staying concealed in broad daylight. She had to get a move on while she still had that advantage.

Springing into action, she located her shoes next to the bed and heaved a sigh. Her cute beige suede loafers were stained with dirt and who knew what else. Even if she could get them clean, they'd never be the same. She slipped them on, then crossed to give herself a once-over in the freestanding full-length mirror that stood next to what must be a closet.

Ugh. It was even worse than she'd imagined. Her wrinkled silk trousers and snagged Armani sweater made her look like a homeless person with expensive taste.

She examined the cut on her cheek, which wasn't quite as bad as she'd feared. Still, with no makeup to conceal it, people would wonder what had happened to her. Not the kind of attention she needed right now.

She grunted, making a futile attempt to smooth the unkempt hair around her face. Tears of humiliation pressed against her eyes. Had she actually looked this bedraggled last night? With her eye makeup all askew and her lipstick long gone, she looked more raccoon than human. It was a miracle Joe hadn't mistaken her for roadkill and tossed her in the back of his truck along with the rest of the animals.

It suddenly struck her that she'd brought absolutely no personal items with her. No toothbrush. No comb. And the only makeup she carried in her purse was an ineffectual tube of lip gloss. How could she have been so careless as to neglect the basic essentials for taking it on the lam?

She crept across the room, careful not to make the floor creak too loudly under her weight. Slowly, she pulled the door open just enough to allow a look down the hallway. The last thing she needed was to run into that hunky rancher before she'd had a chance to make herself look presentable.

Seeing that the coast was clear, she scampered down the hall, found the bathroom, and quickly shut herself inside.

A weight filled her chest as her eyes darted around the room. The only items on the small counter next to the sink were a toothbrush and toothpaste. A rack inside the clawfoot tub held a bar of soap and some manly looking shampoo.

With the care of a cat burglar, she tugged at the mirror, which opened to reveal a small medicine cabinet. Guilt filled her as she took a quick inventory. Shaving cream. A razor. A box of Band-Aids.

Huh.

Nothing here indicated the presence of a woman. Or any children.

Of course, this was a big house. Obviously, Mrs. Brannon used another bathroom. And that might be true of anyone else living here.

Still . . .

If Joe was married, wouldn't they share a medicine cabinet?

Letting out a huff of annoyance for allowing her mind to go there, she shut the cabinet door. Just because there were masculine items here didn't mean they belonged to Joe. They could belong to a brother. Or a ranch hand.

Or . . . he could be a bachelor living alone with his grandmother.

Shaking off the thought, she moved on with her surveillance.

Next to the small window, a large white cupboard looked promising. She eased it open. A slightly manic chortle came out at the sight of clean blue towels and washcloths. She picked up a cloth and returned to the mirror.

"Really, Carrie?" She spoke softly to her pitiable image. "You couldn't have taken sixty seconds to grab your makeup bag before you fled for your life?" She doused the cloth with warm water and ran it over her face, chiding herself for her concern over her appearance when so much more was at stake.

The truth was, she'd been distracting herself to keep her worries about Lucas at bay. He could be a real dunce, but he was still her little brother, and the thought of him in danger was more than she could stand.

After doing the best she could to make herself pass for human, she swished a dollop of borrowed toothpaste around in her mouth, then met her image once again in the mirror.

A lump formed in her throat, and she blinked back tears. As humiliating as it was, she had no choice but to leave this room. Besides, the smell of coffee had reached her nose. It was either stay holed up indefinitely in a stranger's bathroom, or show her makeup-free face in public.

At least the second option held the promise of breakfast.

Chapter 6

As Carrie made her way downstairs and followed her nose to locate the kitchen, it occurred to her that she hadn't eaten or even had anything to drink since lunch the day before. At that thought, her entire body went limp and her stomach let out a loud protest.

Mrs. Brannon looked up from the table, where she had just set a large platter of what looked to be both pancakes and waffles. A warm smile lit her face. "Good morning, dear. I'll bet you're famished." She waved a bent hand over the bounty of dishes that she must have risen at dawn to prepare. "I didn't know what you would want, so I made some of everything."

She wasn't kidding. Eggs and bacon. Pancakes, waffles, and muffins that were no doubt made with eggs, butter, and milk. Making her way to the table, Carrie felt a rush of guilt. Why hadn't she bothered to mention last night that she was a vegan?

She gulped. "You really didn't have to go to the trouble."

"It's no trouble." Mrs. Brannon batted a tiny hand as she shuffled back to the stove. "I make breakfast every day, anyway. What's one more setting at the table?"

Feeling weak-kneed, Carrie sank into the chair closest to her. *One more setting*, for a total of three. She smiled slightly. Chalk one up to the bachelor-living-with-his-grandma theory.

She reached for a pitcher of orange juice and filled the little glass next to her plate practically to the brim. She downed it, then filled it again, hoping its cold sweetness would sate her sudden bout of low blood sugar.

If Mrs. Brannon thought her behavior rude, she didn't show it. Using both hands, she carried a pot of coffee to the table, then braced the spout on the edge of Carrie's cup and poured the heavenly smelling liquid. "I hope you slept well."

"Like the dead." The words tumbled out of Carrie's mouth before their deeper meaning hit her between the eyes. She bit down on her lower lip so hard she almost yelped in pain.

"I'm glad to hear it." Mrs. Brannon methodically filled the other two cups, like this was just another day. If Joe had shared the details of the previous night with her, she wasn't letting on. In fact, it appeared that taking in stranded motorists and feeding them a breakfast fit for royalty was a daily routine for her.

Carrie jumped at the sound of a door shutting somewhere off to her right. A moment later, Joe entered, looking rugged in jeans and a work shirt.

She blinked in an effort not to stare. The man was even hunkier by the light of day.

He let his gaze rest on her for a long moment, reigniting her painful awareness of her own ratty appearance.

"Joseph." Assessing him, Mrs. Brannon returned the coffee pot to the warming plate. "Did you wipe your feet?"

"Yes, ma'am," he answered, then gave Carrie a half smile that made her heart do a funny *ka-thump*. He took the seat at the head of the table. "Not a day passes that she doesn't ask me that question."

"Someday when I'm gone, you'll miss my pestering." Mrs. Brannon smiled as she approached the table and set a bowl of mixed fruit—thank goodness!—next to Carrie. She took the remaining seat, then reached a hand out to Joe. He clasped it in his much larger one.

Carrie felt a measure of her anxiety ease. There was something about the obvious warmth between the two of them that, irrationally, made her feel safe here.

No sooner had that thought settled than she realized that Mrs. Brannon had extended a hand across the table in her direction as well. Her breath caught in her throat at what seemed like an oddly intimate gesture from someone she'd just met. Then it dawned on her. This was the preamble to the blessing on the food.

She cast a glance at Joe, whose gaze held on his grandmother's hand hovering over the table between them. Was he thinking he needed to spare Carrie from letting him touch her because she'd acted like a scared cat last night, jolting at his every move?

"Grandma, I don't think Carrie—"

"No, it's fine." Carrie flicked a wave that was supposed to reassure but looked more like a wayward fly swat.

She took Mrs. Brannon's hand which, while clearly bent by the arthritis that Joe had mentioned, felt surprisingly strong. Joe gave her a skeptical look, then reached out to her as well. As she allowed his hand to enclose hers, she cast a glance at it.

Sure enough. No ring.

Joe and his grandmother both closed their eyes, and Carrie smiled to herself before doing the same.

A few minutes later, they were fully involved in the meal. No one commented on the fact that she had filled her plate with nothing but fruit and some avocado garnish from the egg platter.

"So . . ." She cleared her throat. "I need to get my car taken care of."

"Already did it."

She stared at Joe, a fork-stabbed strawberry poised halfway between her plate and her mouth. "Did . . . what?"

"Had it towed to Hal's Auto Body in town. He said he'd take a look at the tire as soon as he gets a minute."

"Oh." She sat there, not knowing quite how to respond. It was barely daylight, and he had already rescued her car and spoken to the mechanic? She fumbled for words. "Well . . . thank you." Then panic bubbled in her throat at the thought of what this was going to cost her. "What do I owe you for the tow truck?"

Shoving a forkful of pancake into his mouth, Joe shook his head. He swallowed, then took a swig of coffee before answering. "Hal'll tack that on to his bill. You don't owe me anything."

"Where will you be heading from here, dear?" Mrs. Brannon's tone suggested an assumption that Carrie was on some kind of fun adventure; one with an actual itinerary.

"I don't know . . . exactly. I'm more or less taking it as it comes."

A fleeting look passed between her hosts, which she could easily have missed had she not been brutally aware of her own lack of disclosure.

"Oh!" Mrs. Brannon moved to stand, as if something important had just occurred to her. "You're both out of coffee." The meaningful glance she gave Joe as she stood wasn't lost on Carrie.

Setting his fork down, Joe lowered his voice just enough to imply confidentiality. "No use tiptoeing around this. You're in some kind of a bind."

"I don't—"

"Hear me out." He gently held up a hand to stop her argument. "This trip you're on was obviously spur of the moment. No suitcase. No change of clothes."

A blush hit her cheeks and she lowered her head in shame.

"I'm not saying this to make you self-conscious. Whatever's happening in your life is your business. It's just that . . ." He turned his chair slightly toward her, resting his elbows on his knees in an effort to encourage eye contact. "I get the feeling that you might be short on cash. Is that true?"

She met his gaze, surprised that he'd mentioned *that*, of all things. As if the part about her thinking she'd killed a man were the lesser of her problems.

Not quite knowing where this was going or how much she wanted to say, she simply nodded.

"Well," Mrs. Brannon had made her return trek to the table, and was now busy refilling their cups. "I happen to have a suggestion that might be a blessing all the way around."

Joe's brown eyes narrowed. "Grandma . . ."

"Oh, Joseph. We might as well admit that you've told me everything." She poured what remained of the coffee then turned her focus to Carrie. "I prayed about it last night and when I woke up this morning, I had a notion that we should invite you to stay."

Joe's eyebrows shot up and he opened his mouth like he was about to protest, but Carrie beat him to it.

"Stay? But . . . why?"

With a light shrug of her thin shoulders, Mrs. Brannon started her slow amble back toward the sink. "It occurs to me that we could pay you to work as my helper."

Carrie and Joe traded a puzzled look that said he'd had no more inkling of this being in the offing than she had. Working his jaw, he leaned back and tossed his napkin onto his plate.

As much as Carrie appreciated the suggestion, there was no way she could accept. She needed to find out what was going on with her brother, and she had a life to get back to. Not to mention that Joe was clearly opposed to the idea. No, she'd have to find another solution.

"Thank you for your kindness." She pushed back her chair. "But I'll be fine."

Her response was met with an awkward pause, filled only by the ticking of the clock above the door. She stood, not at all sure what to expect next.

Rising to his feet as well, Joe broke the silence. "If you want, I could take you into town now. See about your car and maybe help you get a few supplies." He made an ambiguous gesture, indicating her lack of fresh clothing and personal items. "Whatever you might need."

Feeling her chest tighten with a vague sense of foreboding, she nodded absently. Joe was right. She needed things. Not just the hygiene items, but food and gas. She'd have to use her credit cards and trust that it wouldn't give away her location.

Propelled by a surge of queasiness, she took a step backward. "I'll just go up and get my purse." She turned tail and quickly beat it out of the room.

Chapter 7

The second Joe heard Carrie's footfall on the staircase, he crossed to Grandma and leaned a fist on the counter. "What are you thinking?"

She glanced up from the sink, which she had started to fill with sudsy water. "What do you mean?"

"I mean, we still don't know what she's running from. And you go inviting trouble."

"Joseph. Need I remind you that she said no."

"That's not the point. You should have talked to me about it first. We both live here."

"Oh, really?" Turning to him, she raised a brow and plunked a hand on her narrow hip. "In the same way that you should have consulted me before bringing her here in the first place?"

"That was different. It was an emergency. And it was just for one night."

"I trusted your judgment on the matter, and you should trust mine." She started for the table, and he followed. "If there's one thing I've learned in all my years of living, it's that when the good Lord gives me peace on what sounds like a crazy notion, I have to trust that peace."

"And you're feeling peace about this?" He picked up the platter that was still mostly full of pancakes and waffles, and took it to the counter. "About offering sanctuary to a woman who might be either crazy or on the run from the law."

"Yes." Her head bobbed decisively as she retrieved the empty plates. "And I don't think the problem is either of those things."

"I hope you're right." Shaking his head, he huffed out a long breath. "Still, I can't say I'm sorry she declined." He paused, not quite sure how he wanted to word this next question. "So . . . what were you thinking you would have been hiring her to do, exactly?"

"Oh, you know." She set the plates next to the sink then batted her hand. "A million little things."

"You wanna get a little more specific on the job description?"

An audible breath puffed out and her shoulders slumped slightly. "I think it's time that you and I both face the fact that I'm not getting any younger."

He held his breath, waiting for her to say more. When he realized that was all he was going to get, he sent up a quick prayer of thanks. Even that small admission of her growing need for assistance lifted a burden from him. Finally, she had opened the door for this discussion.

He placed a hand on her shoulder and kissed her temple.

She shooed him away. "Get on with you. You should give Jeremy a call before Carrie comes back down. Maybe he can find something out before you have to send her on her way."

"Right." He reached behind the cookie jar for his phone and pushed the On button as he stepped into the mud room. He never had gotten used to keeping this thing with him, the way everyone said he should. Besides, cell service out here was spotty at best, and he didn't exactly feel the need to be easy to reach. If Grandma needed him, she just rang the bell on the back porch. That system suited him just fine.

He stepped outside, thinking this conversation should be had where there was no chance that Carrie might overhear. Even if he'd never see her again after today, he didn't want to leave her with the impression that she couldn't trust strangers who had her best interests at heart.

After taking a final opportunity to freshen up before the next leg of her journey, Carrie looked at her image in the bathroom mirror. Who was she kidding? She had absolutely nowhere to turn and no one she could go to for help. Lucas was her only family. The friendships she'd made in Seattle were basically superficial. Ever since her parents had died, she'd avoided forming any close bonds with anyone for fear of losing them. And what had that gotten her? An empty life with no one to even notice she was gone.

Of course, the other agents at her office might notice. But to them, her disappearance would only be grist for the gossip mill. None of them would be willing to actually get involved if she reached out for help.

The tears finally came, and she wilted into a slumped position on the edge of the tub. As flawed as this plan was, she felt safe here. Staying for a few days would at least buy her some time to figure out what to do, and to earn enough cash to do it.

What other choice did she have?

Joe leaned against the porch railing, gazing out at the cattle he'd unloaded that morning in the back field. He'd just given Jeremy—the town sheriff, and his best buddy since childhood—the lowdown on Carrie.

"Didn't tell you her last name, huh?" Jeremy's tone was all business.

"I'm not even sure she gave me her real *first* name. I'm telling you, something's not right."

"Let me run these plates and I'll get back to you. Okay if I send a text?"

Joe huffed out agitation at his friend, who was forever trying to yank him kicking and screaming into the age of modern technology. "Whatever's easiest."

"Great. Keep your phone on you in case I need to break it to you that you've been harboring a fugitive."

"Or protecting a witness?"

"Yeah. Or that."

Joe ended the call and stuck the phone in his shirt pocket, pondering which of those options would be worse. Yeah. It was just as well that she'd turned down Grandma's job offer. Life was complicated enough already.

And yet . . .

No. He shrugged off the misty sense of destiny that had gnawed at him ever since he'd met her. That feeling of something not quite coincidental but more God-ordained about what seemed to be a random encounter with a stranger. And the pinch of regret at the inevitability of their parting ways forever.

When he clomped through the mud room and into the kitchen, the two women stepped out of a hug that, from the look of unease on Carrie's face, had to have been initiated by his overly affectionate grandmother.

"Joe." Grandma turned to him, beaming. "You'll never guess what's happened."

"Yeah?" A confusing mix of dread and relief hit him squarely in the chest as he looked at Carrie's tentative smile.

"I changed my mind." Her face creased like she expected he wouldn't be pleased. "I decided to stay."

He nodded. Yeah, she might have decided all right, but she sure didn't look any too happy about it.

Chapter 8

After Joe left Carrie at the Rockford department store with instructions to buy whatever she needed on his store credit—which she would then earn back as Mrs. Brannon's helper—she had spent the better part of an hour speed shopping.

Now, as she exited the store dressed in brand-new jeans, sneakers, and a T-shirt which proclaimed her affection for the Big Sky Country, and carrying a couple of bags filled with more shirts, socks, and undies, she drew in a satisfied breath. At least her brief stay at the ranch would be more comfortable to dress for than office life.

Joe had told her that, in addition to checking on her car, he had a few errands of his own to run. He'd pointed out the drugstore across the street and promised he'd meet her there.

She stepped to the curb and looked both ways, which seemed silly considering that the road leading out of town was visible for quite some distance and there wasn't a car to be seen in either direction. She crossed the street and angled toward the drugstore.

A young woman standing behind the cash register barely looked up from the magazine she was reading when Carrie entered. *Interesting*. So far, no one had seemed curious about her in the slightest. This didn't seem like a town that would get a lot of tourists, but maybe strangers just passing through weren't all that unusual. She found that comforting. The last thing she wanted was to stand out.

Being mindful of the debt she was accumulating—how much were they going to pay her per hour, anyway?—she picked out some basic makeup, face wash, and shampoo. A travel size toothbrush and toothpaste seemed optimistic, but she found the thought of being a fugitive long enough to go through a full-size tube disheartening.

After grabbing a package of combs and a small deodorant, she scanned the room for anything resembling an electronics section. A sign in the front corner declaring the presence of "Phones and Cameras" looked promising and she hurried toward it.

Hallelujah. They had one of the type of charger she needed for Lucas's phone. She snapped it up, as if someone else might suddenly swoop in and claim it. Considering the thin layer of dust that coated the package, that fear seemed superfluous.

At least now she'd be able to charge the phone and, hopefully, get a message to Lucas that she'd lost her own phone and he could call her on his.

Dropping the charger into her basket with the other items, she reviewed her mental shopping list. That should about do it. Maybe by the time she paid, Joe would be there to meet her.

She stepped out into the main aisle, then stopped short at the sight of a man standing at the front counter speaking to the clerk. Her stomach buckled, and she scooted back out of view, then peered around a display of cold medicine to get a better look at him.

His conversation with the clerk was an indecipherable hum, but he didn't seem to be making a purchase. It looked like he was questioning her. Asking directions, or . . . something else.

Carrie's heart raced. The man was medium height, with dark hair and a ruddy complexion. He wore old jeans and an untucked plaid-flannel shirt. Not familiar to her, really, but not exactly unfamiliar either. She hadn't gotten a good look at her attacker. Could this possibly be him? Was he asking around town for her?

Making a broad gesture with his arm, he turned slightly and Carrie dipped back into the aisle. She stood there for what felt like a full minute—trapped-rat style. Sweat beaded her forehead and her breath came in such short bursts she thought she might pass out. What was she going to—

"Get everything you need?"

She whirled around to face Joe, who looked startled by her reaction. Realizing that it was him, she nearly folded in humiliation and relief.

"Whoa . . . sorry." He held out a hand to steady her. "You okay?"

"Yeah, I . . ." She took a quick glance around the endcap, just in time to see the flannel-shirt man leave the building. "I guess I'm a little jumpy."

"Obviously." The word held an edge of derision, but his face looked concerned. "I maybe shouldn't have left you all alone so soon after . . . whatever happened to you last night."

She eyed him narrowly. Did he not believe her? Sure, there had been no solid evidence of the attack in the motel room, but the slice in her tire was real enough. He'd seen that with his own eyes.

He reached out to relieve her of her shopping bags. "So, about your tire."

She took in a breath. How did he keep reading her thoughts like that?

"Hal says there's no way to fix it." With an apologetic shrug, he started toward the front counter. "It's going to take a few days to get a new one. So, I guess it's a good thing you changed your mind about leaving today."

"I guess it is." She waited until they had paid for her items and headed for the door before she continued. "Did Hal say anything about what he thought happened to my tire?"

"Just that it looked like a stab. A big gash about three inches long that went clean through. Like someone didn't want you going anywhere anytime soon."

A chill ran through her as they stepped outside. She shrank back a little, taking in the entire length of both sides of the street. All she saw were a couple of kids on bikes and a man in overalls hefting some sacks into the back of a truck.

"You okay?" He spoke softly, dipping his head like he wanted her to look at him. "If there's something you want to talk about—"

"No. I just . . ." What could she tell him? So far, she didn't seem to have much credibility with him and the last thing she wanted was for him to contact the authorities. "I feel a little woozy, I guess."

"Not surprised."

"What do you mean?"

"I figure you must be working up an appetite about now. You didn't eat a whole lot at breakfast. You want to get some lunch? It's on me." He commenced walking up the sidewalk. "I'm not promising anything fancy, but our diner has the best meatloaf sandwich money can buy."

"That's great." As much as she tried to act casual, her voice still held an uncontrollable quiver. "What I'd really love is a salad."

"Rabbit food, huh?" A slight smirk seemed good natured. "They have that too."

"Sounds good, then." Feeling vulnerable, she couldn't help but check out each store window as they passed. But the guy in the flannel shirt had vanished.

"You looking for something?"

"What? No." Why was she so amped up? That guy probably had nothing to do with her. She needed to calm down and keep her wits about her. "Just thinking what a cute town this is."

"Cute?" He chuckled. "I guess you could call it that."

"You always live here?" Relieved to have the spotlight moved off her, she remained on the alert as they walked.

"'Cept for the four years I spent at Montana State."

"Oh?" She had to admit that her regard for him rose a notch at the notion that he'd gone to college. Did that make her a snob?

He lifted a smile. "Don't look so surprised."

Busted. "I . . . I'm not."

He cocked an eyebrow at her.

"Okay. Maybe a little. I just didn't realize that people went to college to learn ranching. I thought it was something you just—"

"Know how to do?"

"Yeah. In a way. I guess I assumed it's passed down through the generations."

"True. I learned ranching from my grandpa. And my dad, before he passed."

"I'm so sorry."

"Water under the bridge." He shrugged. "We lost him and my mom when I was eight. A semi swerved to avoid a deer on the interstate, and it hit them instead."

"Oh, my . . . That's so awful."

"Yeah. Fortunately, my grandparents took me in without missing a beat. I couldn't have asked for better people to raise me so, all in all, I feel pretty blessed. How about you?"

"Me?" Her stomach buckled. Had he told her that story as bait for his next fishing excursion? "I'm pretty boring. My parents have passed too. Only it wasn't quite so sudden. They both worked for Arnaco. It's a chemical company in California."

"And, that made them sick?"

"Well, they and several of their coworkers wound up mysteriously dying from lung cancer. I was eighteen. The company. . ." She swallowed. ". . . they swear they're not responsible, like that's just some kind of weird coincidence. Anyway, it's like you said. Water under the bridge."

"That's a pretty nasty bridge to have to cross, though. I'm really sorry."

She blinked back the sadness surrounding this topic that seemed never to diminish. "Me too. Anyway . . ." She looked around for something to inspire a lighter mood. All she saw on this sleepy little street were dusty old buildings, most of which were in need of a paint job, that housed mundane-looking businesses. Not much to stimulate scintillating conversation. "What do you do in this town for fun?"

"Nice way to take the focus off yourself, Miss . . ." He stopped in front of a splintery wooden door with a screened top half. ". . . Carrie-with-no-last-name."

She blew out a breath. So, he was changing his interrogation tactic from questioning to quasi-flirting. Impressive. She'd have to stay on high alert lest she be caught off guard by his charm and cunning. Still, she couldn't deny that in spite of the circumstances, she was actually sort of having a nice time with him.

The sound of cheerful conversation along with the smell of greasy food bombarded her senses as he opened the screen door and waited for her to pass through it. She entered, surprised that his show of gallantry felt refreshing. Back home, men were afraid that a gesture like this would get them slapped with some sort of discrimination charge. Here, it made her feel respected. Protected, even.

Once inside the light, cheerful diner, the tightness in her muscles eased. Unlike the precisely planned eateries she was used to in the city, this place almost felt like they'd just walked into someone's home. An assortment of jackets and hats—mostly of the cowboy variety—hung from hooks just inside the door. Candid photos lined the wall leading to the front counter, where an old-fashioned cash register sat next to a glass case filled with turquoise jewelry. The room, which was larger than it looked from outside, was crammed with mismatched tables, each draped with a different pattern of tablecloth, and encircled by a hodgepodge mix of wooden chairs.

Not even the country music playing softly through a couple of old speakers close to the ceiling put her off. In fact, instead of feeling tacky, as she would have expected, the place felt comfortable and welcoming. Like coming home.

Several heads turned as they walked in, much to her chagrin. But everyone simply smiled or lifted a hand in greeting then returned their attention to their food or conversation.

"Well hey, Joe." A woman of around forty, dressed in jeans and a short-sleeved blouse, and carrying a pot of coffee, appeared in front of them and grabbed a couple of menus from a holder on the edge of the front counter.

"Hey, Mill." Joe responded. "This is Carrie. She'll be helping out around the ranch for a little while."

"Nice to meet you, Carrie." Nodding in approval, Mill—or Millie, according to her name tag—gave her a friendly smile then led the way to a table next to the front window. "Here you go, you two." She set the menus down and started to fill the cups sitting there without asking if they wanted coffee. "Specials are on the front. Today's pie is lemon meringue, but it's going fast so I'd advise you speak up."

Joe cast Carrie a *want-pie?* look as they settled into their seats.

"None for me, thanks." She decided against giving any further explanation of her dietary restrictions, not wanting to inspire curiosity. Best to avoid that kind of attention if at all possible.

Turning her chair slightly so she could see both ways down the street, she heaved a breath and picked up her menu. The sooner they ate, the sooner she could get back to the ranch and start planning her next move.

Chapter 9

Try as he might, Joe couldn't manage to get Carrie to relax enough to open up to him. Even now as she sat there studying the diner menu and making small talk, she couldn't seem to stop sneaking looks out the window, like she was afraid someone out there was going to spot her before she spotted them.

Millie swung by and refilled their coffee. "You two ready?"

Carrie surrendered her menu, without having even really looked at it. "I'll just have the house salad. No croutons."

"Dressing?"

"Oh . . . uh . . . just some lemon wedges."

Joe frowned. He'd been on dates with women who tried to pretend they didn't ever eat, but Carrie seemed too smart for that kind of nonsense. Could be that the stress of her situation was doing a number on her stomach. He decided not to press it.

"Meatloaf sandwich, please." He handed his menu to Millie. "And that pie sounds mighty good, if you've got any left."

"Already set aside a slice for you." With a wink, Millie headed to the kitchen to put in their order.

"You know—" Easing back a little, Carrie folded her arms and studied him. "—you never answered my question."

"Which question was that?"

Her gaze drifted to the window again, only this time it seemed more casual. "What do you do for fun in this town?"

Just as he leaned his elbows on the table and was about to answer, his shirt pocket buzzed. He let out a little groan at the interruption, which he would have ignored had he not been so anxious to hear from Jeremy on the license plate results.

"'Scuse me." He reached into his pocket, hating to be one of *those people*. "I don't usually—"

"No, it's fine." She batted an unconcerned hand, like she was used to being cast aside in favor of an incoming text, then turned to stare out the window again.

Hoping for some kind of good news, but having no idea what that might be, he clicked on his phone and pulled up the message from Jeremy.

Car registered to Carrie Amelia Yost, Seattle. No criminal record.

That made him smile. It wasn't much, but at least it wasn't bad news. He tapped out a quick response.

Thanks, bud. I owe you.

As he moved to put his phone away, it buzzed again. He gave it a quick look.

Saw you walking into the diner. She's a babe!

He rolled his eyes, then returned the phone to his pocket. When he looked up again, Carrie was studying him.

"Everything okay?"

Nodding, he leaned forward. "Appears to be."

"Good." Mimicking his movements, she unfolded her arms and leaned on the table. "Now, back to my question."

He smiled, trying to recall the last time he had actually done anything just for fun. "Well, let's see now. There's a rodeo in August."

"Uh-huh."

"The ladies in town put on a cake walk every fall to raise funds for the church."

"Okay."

"At Christmastime, we all decorate that big tree over there. The one that sits on the corner across from the post office in the little park."

"That's nice. But what about now?"

"Now?"

"You know. It's the beginning of summer. What would you do if you went out with friends? Or on a date, maybe?"

He squinted. Was there some kind of underlying motive to that question? Or was that just wishful thinking on his part? He decided to assume the latter. Why would she care if he was dating anyone, when she'd made it clear that her time here was short?

"Well, there's not much to the town, obviously. If you want to go someplace nice to get dinner, you pretty much have to drive for an hour to get to Luxton. There's a real nice restaurant there. And a movie theatre. In the summer, they open the playhouse for live shows."

"Sounds nice."

"It is. Around Rockford, there's always horseback riding. Hiking. Inner tubing down the river."

"Getting coffee at the diner?" Taking a sip from her cup, she eyed him over its ridge.

"Yeah. That pretty much rounds out the list of local dating activities." As soon as he said it, he felt a flush at the implication that she might have thought he meant for this to be a date. He hadn't intended to mislead her, and he hoped she hadn't taken it that way. Still, if he was inclined to take up dating again, this wouldn't be a bad way to start.

"Joe."

Caught off guard by the female voice coming from behind him, he turned to see Valerie wiping her hands on her jeans and walking toward them from the kitchen.

He looked at Carrie, whose pretty blue eyes were filled with question marks as they moved from Valerie to him and back again.

Hoo boy. How to handle this?

Carrie tried not to stare at the young-Ava-Gardner lookalike eagerly approaching Joe. Or at Joe himself, whose face had become a study in neutrality.

The woman wore jeans—who didn't around here?—and a form-fitting plaid shirt with the sleeves casually rolled up. Her brunette hair had been pulled into the kind of messy bun that on Carrie always wound up so . . . well, messy. But on this woman, it seemed almost elegant.

"Hey, Valerie." Joe gave her a nod, along with what looked like a tight smile. "You making a delivery?"

"Yeah." Reaching their table, Valerie jabbed a thumb in the direction of the kitchen, then tucked her fingertips into the pockets of her jeans. Her country-girl beauty—probably a product of fortunate genes and a lot of fresh air—would have been downright maddening if she hadn't seemed so unassuming. "I didn't expect to see you in town today."

"We had some things come up." Joe looked pleasant enough, but Carrie detected the tiniest strain in his voice. He lifted a hand across the table. "This is Carrie. She'll be helping out at the ranch for a while."

"Oh . . ." While the smile remained on Valerie's lips, it vanished from her eyes. What was going on between these two? "It's nice to meet you. I'm Valerie."

Carrie sensed that Valerie wanted to add an explanation of who she was, or—more to the point—who she was *to Joe*. But she didn't.

"Nice to meet you too." Not wanting to either appear rude or encourage conversation, Carrie lifted her coffee cup and homed in on it, as if drinking from it required her full focus.

Valerie returned her attention to Joe. "So, you all ready for Saturday?"

Carrie's muddled brain stumbled. Everything had been so helter-skelter that she scarcely remembered what day of the week this was. *Tuesday*. So, what would be happening on Saturday?

"We will be." Joe swung his head from side to side, more like he was getting the kinks out of his neck than answering her question. "Grandma does most of the prep work. All I have to do is show up and man the barbecue."

Barbecue? So, it was some kind of social event. Why hadn't he mentioned this when she'd prodded him about what they do for fun here? Maybe he assumed she'd be gone by then. Or hoped she'd be.

And maybe he already had a date . . .

Seeming satisfied with his answer, Valerie turned her berry-blue eyes back on Carrie. "You just passing through, or will you be staying a while?"

Carrie's heart rattled in her chest. How could she answer in a way that wouldn't encourage any follow-up?

"We'll see." Her mouth clamped shut and she turned her attention to the street outside, to where precisely nothing was going on.

She was terrible! Not only did Valerie seem genuinely friendly, but she'd been the first person in town, apart from Joe and Mrs. Brannon, who'd actually shown any interest in her. And here Carrie was treating her with callous disinterest just because she didn't want to have to answer any personal questions.

"Well, I should get going." The lightheartedness in Valerie's tone clearly served as a cover for something else. Disappointment. Suspicion, maybe?

Carrie felt an urge to make up for her contribution to this poor woman's obvious dis-ease. She looked at her, smiling. "It was really nice to meet you."

"You too." Valerie nodded, looking like she meant it. "I'm sure I'll see you again."

Valerie and Joe exchanged goodbyes, and she headed back toward the kitchen.

As soon as she walked away, Joe turned his attention to his coffee as if Valerie's visit had been no big deal. But Carrie suspected otherwise. Out of all the patrons in this rather busy diner, Valerie had zeroed in on him. And why had her presence spelled an end to the easy feeling between Carrie and Joe?

Admittedly, she had limited experience with actual relationships, but she'd dated enough, and certainly *flirted* enough, to recognize chemistry. She and Joe had definitely been fanning a flirtatious flame. But Valerie's arrival had served as a bucket of cold water, dousing the spark.

She sighed. Somehow, she'd wound up in the middle of something she clearly had no place in. The sooner she extracted herself from it, the better it would be for everyone.

Chapter 10

"**W**ould you grab that small saucepan for me, dear?" Mrs. Brannon aimed a gnarled finger at an impressive collection of pans hanging from a metal rack over the butcher-block kitchen island.

Wiping her hands on a towel, Carrie admired the assortment of pans. "That's some serious cookware." She freed the pan from its hook, surprised by its weight. "My set at home seems so cheap compared to these."

"Cheap cookware will only frustrate you. Always use cast iron." The older woman took the pan from Carrie and placed it on the stove. "You get the best results."

"I've heard it's hard to cook with."

"Well then, you've been listening to the wrong people."

Returning to the tomatoes she'd been chopping for the salad she'd heartily volunteered to make, Carrie marveled at how at home she felt here. Spending the afternoon in the kitchen with her hostess had been unexpectedly relaxing. While Carrie enjoyed cooking, she seldom went to this much trouble to prepare a meal. Even when she entertained, which was rare, she took as many shortcuts as she could.

But, while she appreciated the distraction, her need to get in touch with Lucas was never far from her mind. As soon as she finished the salad, she'd excuse herself to check on his phone, which she'd left charging upstairs.

A vague plan had formed. The only friend that Lucas talked about was someone named Zander, a guy he knew from work. It seemed likely that his number would be on Lucas's phone and that he would be willing to get a message to him if he could.

Mrs. Brannon removed a mason jar from the heavy-duty refrigerator, which clearly still worked but appeared to have been there since the days when it was probably referred to as an icebox.

Seeing what the jar contained, Carrie almost laughed. "Don't tell me you actually churn your own butter."

"You haven't *had* butter until you've made your own. Besides—" She lowered her voice. "—it would be an insult to our cows if I used store-bought."

Carrie chuckled. "You wouldn't want to insult the cows."

"Never." Considering the arthritic bent to her hands, she unscrewed the lid with surprising dexterity. "We need to melt a spoonful or so of this over a very low heat. Is that timer about ready to go off?" Mrs. Brannon waved a hand in the direction of the ticking metal cube that looked like it had served this kitchen for probably half a century.

"About two more minutes." Carrie reported as she peered through the window of the oven, watching the dinner rolls she'd helped Mrs. Brannon create turn a perfect golden brown. The heavenly smell was almost enough to convince her to make an exception to her no dairy or eggs discipline. Almost.

Mrs. Brannon lifted the lid off a large pot on the stove, augmenting the hearty aroma that had permeated the kitchen for the past couple of hours. Carrie had fully intended to mention her vegan lifestyle before they got too far into the dinner preparations, but when her hostess had started chopping hunks of beef, she'd been so involved in recounting their family history that Carrie hadn't wanted to interrupt.

"Joe is so much like my late husband, Henry," Mrs. Brannon casually commented as she removed a spoon from a drawer.

"Really?" Carrie smiled, filing away every tidbit of information she could collect on Joe, even though she knew her undeniable crush on him was pointless. "How so?"

"Well . . . in lots of ways, really." She dipped the spoon into the stew. "But when it comes to food, Joe's a meat-and-potatoes man, just like his grandfather."

Carrie simply nodded at that. So much for compatibility.

"He's very easy to please." Mrs. Brannon lifted the spoon to her mouth, but retracted it as another thought took precedence. "Trouble is, he tells me everything I cook is perfect."

"And that's a problem, how?"

"I never know if I should believe him. I'd rather have honesty than platitudes, wouldn't you?"

The knot that had been ever present in Carrie's stomach for the past several days tightened. "Honesty is important."

"Agreed." Finally, Mrs. Brannon tasted the stew then looked thoughtful. Making a contemplative humming sound, she took another spoon from the drawer and held it out to Carrie. "So I trust you to tell me if this needs anything."

Carrie released a breath. "It smells great. But, in all honesty . . . I don't really eat meat."

Mrs. Brannon looked up, her brow furrowing. "You don't like meat?"

"Well . . . it's not that I don't *like* it, exactly. I just choose not to eat it. I'm a vegan"

"Oh." Still holding the spoon, her eyebrows pinched together. "What does that mean, dear?"

"It means I don't eat anything that comes from an animal."

"I see. Like a vegetarian."

"Sort of. But vegetarians will eat dairy and eggs, which vegans don't."

"You don't eat meat, dairy, or eggs?" Her befuddled gaze grew slightly distant. "Oh dear. No wonder you barely ate this morning."

"I'm so sorry. I should have mentioned it sooner. I just didn't want to be a bother."

Putting the spoon back in the drawer, Mrs. Brannon shook her head. "Telling people what you need is never being a bother. Now . . ." Plunking a hand on one of her thin hips, she looked around thoughtfully. "What exactly *can* you eat?"

"Oh, lots of things." Trying to sound lighthearted, Carrie picked up the salad and took it to the table. "Any kind of vegetable. And fruit. Nuts and seeds. Grains. I really don't want this to be a problem for you. I'm used to working around it."

"Nonsense. You're our guest. You shouldn't have to work around anything." She thought for a moment. "How about a nice bowl of oatmeal?"

"That sounds delicious."

"Coming right up."

"With no milk, of course."

Mrs. Brannon's face puckered, as if the thought appalled her. "No wonder you're so thin."

Carrie chuckled to herself. Her diminutive hostess was definitely calling the kettle black with her allegation of thinness. But Carrie knew she meant well.

A tinny *buzz* sent Carrie's heart into her throat, which seemed ridiculous when she saw that it was just the timer going off. Mrs. Brannon took a couple of mitts from a hook on the nearby wall and opened the oven.

"Those look incredible." Carrie crossed back to the counter and watched as Mrs. Brannon removed the pan from the oven and set it on a cooling rack.

"But you can't eat any?" Mrs. Brannon blinked, like the thought struck her as tragic. "I can't imagine a life without bread."

"Oh, there are lots of good vegan breads." She picked up the stack of plates and silverware that Mrs. Brannon had stacked on the counter, and headed for the table. "Maybe we can find a recipe."

"That's a good idea. We'll do that." Mrs. Brannon glanced up at the clock. "Look at the time. I should go call Joe in for dinner."

Was it really that late? Carrie checked for herself, seeing that it wasn't quite five. Back home, she'd still be working. Meeting with a client, or getting ready to face rush hour traffic. She wouldn't even be thinking about dinner for a couple more hours. But her appetite told her that adjusting wouldn't be difficult. That salad at the diner had been adequate, but not very substantial.

The sound of the back door gave her a tiny jolt of anticipation. A moment later, Joe appeared, his skin glistening with the sweat of a good day's work.

She couldn't help but toss him a smile as she distributed the three plates around the table. "Did you wipe your feet?"

An appreciative grin graced his handsome features. "I see she's getting you trained already."

His grandma gave him a playful backhand to the stomach. "Don't sass the hands that feed you."

"Two against one." He held up his palms in surrender. "I see how it's going to be around here."

Carrie gulped in air as she finished placing the silverware next to the plates. Surely, he hadn't meant to imply that she might be staying a while.

Mrs. Brannon seemed unfazed by his insinuation. "You must be hungry if you didn't even wait for the dinner bell."

"Who can work with the smell of your beef stew in the air?" Crossing to the sink, he inhaled deeply, then tossed Carrie a look as she returned to the counter to pick up the bowls Mrs. Brannon had set out. "You haven't tasted beef stew till you've had my grandma's."

"Joe, dear." Mrs. Brannon had gotten out a pan and a box of oats. "She doesn't eat that. She's a vegan."

"A *vegan*." Washing his hands up to the elbow, he cast an amused look over his shoulder. He turned the water off, and grabbed a towel. "You do realize you're living on a cattle ranch?"

She shrugged her brows. "At least the cows don't have to be afraid of me."

"I'll be sure to let them know."

Noting that his pre-Valerie flirtatious tone had returned, Carrie felt her cheeks redden. That, combined with a growing sense of urgency to catch up with Lucas, propelled her toward the door. "I just need to run upstairs. I'll be right back."

Once in her room, she made a beeline for the table next to the bed, where she'd left the phone. She tugged it free from the plug, then pushed the button on the back and brought the screen to life. It glowed a cheerful blue, but the image of a white padlock in the center of the screen sent her brain into a tailspin. Below it were instructions to "Enter Pin Number."

She stared at it in disbelief. Why would he lock his phone?

Her stomach clenched. In movies, people always guessed things like pin numbers and passwords, but she had no idea where to even begin.

Trying not to cry, she tossed the phone onto the bed. Even if she had the ability to guess at this, now wasn't the time. It wouldn't be fair to make her hosts wait while she played detective.

Her heart felt heavy as she left her room and started for the stairs. She'd been set on accessing Lucas's contacts to find someone who could check on him. What was she going to do now?

Chapter 11

The next morning after breakfast, Carrie followed Mrs. Brannon out to the expansive front porch. She held two full mugs of coffee, while her hostess carried a large pad of paper and a pen.

"I'm so pleased that we're getting organized." Mrs. Brannon braced herself against the arm of one of the two white rocking chairs that flanked a small table, then lowered herself into it. "It will be easier for both of us if we're clear on the expectations for your job."

Carrie paused, letting her gaze linger on the land that stretched out as far as the eye could see. This place felt so peaceful. Yet, with no houses for miles around, she couldn't help but feel vulnerable. What if that man found her again?

The previous night after dinner, she'd tried all the possible pin numbers she could think of for Lucas's phone, but nothing had unlocked it. For now, that seemed like a lost cause. Her next best option would be to borrow the phone here to call his workplace, which opened at eight—nine o'clock here in Montana. She checked her watch. She still had a few minutes.

"Is everything all right, dear?"

Startling from her thoughts, Carrie realized she hadn't even moved out of the doorway.

"Oh . . . yes. Fine." Stepping fully onto the porch, she eased the old wooden screen door shut behind her.

After setting the mugs down on the table, she sat in the second rocking chair and glanced over at the paper in Mrs. Brannon's lap. Across the top, she had scrolled "Carrie's Job Duties."

A pang of guilt wove through her. These people were being so kind. Even though there wasn't much she could tell them about her situation, she owed it to them to be as honest as possible.

"I don't know how many days I'll be staying. I just need to earn enough money to . . ." She hesitated. How could she explain without revealing any actual details? ". . . get my act together."

Mrs. Brannon nodded, her face scrunching slightly at the vague turn of phrase. "Well, anything you can do to help out will be appreciated."

"And I'm grateful for the opportunity." Taking a sip of fortifying coffee, she tipped her head toward the pad of paper. "I guess this will make it easier for you to hire someone permanently if you've already figured out what you want them to do."

"Yes ... that's true." The older woman's eyes turned liquid, like something had saddened her. But whatever it was, she snapped herself out of it. "We'll just think about that when the time comes, won't we."

With forced cheer, Carrie nodded.

"First things first." Mrs. Brannon held up her pen, ready to write. "I hope you like doing laundry."

Carrie let out a chuckle, thinking of how good she was at putting off doing that task back home. "I don't know if 'like' is the word I'd use, but I'm happy to do it."

"We have a chute for the dirty laundry, but carrying everything back up from the basement once it's clean and folded is getting harder for me to manage."

"Your laundry room is in the basement? Have you talked to Joe about moving it to the main floor of the house?"

"Is that possible?"

"Anything's possible. Maybe he could put a stacking washer and dryer in the mud room."

"What a clever idea. You're earning your keep already."

At the sound of an engine, they both looked up to see a forest-green pickup truck appear over the rise of the driveway.

"Oh my." Mrs. Brannon's eyes widened. "Is it Wednesday already?"

"Are you expecting someone?"

"We get our produce delivery every week at this time."

As the truck pulled closer to the house, Carrie made out the words "Hayes Family Farm" in a cheery, colorful script on its side. It ground to a stop next to Joe's truck, and the driver got out. Carrie sat up a little straighter. It was Valerie.

"Morning, ladies," Valerie called out as she started up the walk.

"Good morning, dear," Mrs. Brannon replied. "I hope you brought enough apples for the pies I promised Gus and Jimmy."

"The boys will not be disappointed."

Valerie smiled sweetly, and Carrie could have sworn she had on lipstick, something that had been lacking yesterday.

Mrs. Brannon leaned on one arm of her chair. "Carrie, dear, this is Valerie Hayes."

Hayes? So, she apparently worked for her family's farm. That explained her presence in the back of the diner.

Carrie smiled. "We met when Joe and I were in town yesterday."

"Did you?" Grandma's lips pursed ever so slightly. "That boy doesn't tell me anything."

Carrie couldn't help but wonder why she would consider that piece of information important enough to share, but she kept her curiosity to herself.

"Good to see you again." Joining them on the porch, Valerie nodded to Carrie, then spoke to Mrs. Brannon. "I've got the first tomatoes of the season. The onions you wanted for the burgers. And lettuce. Plus some early potatoes."

"Wonderful. I'll be able to make my potato salad for Saturday."

Valerie leaned against the porch railing in the manner of someone who felt right at home there. "It wouldn't be the Shadow Ridge Ranch barbecue without your famous potato salad."

Carrie started to put the pieces together. When she and Joe had returned from town, she'd noticed the name "Shadow Ridge Ranch" in big metal letters over the gate to their property. So, they were hosting this barbecue?

Hoping to appear more helpful than nosy, she prodded. "You're having a barbecue on Saturday?"

Mrs. Brannon let out a breath. "Don't tell me Joe didn't mention that to you?"

She shook her head.

"That boy . . ."

Valerie chimed in quickly. "It's the social event of the season."

"Every year, we throw a barbecue on the first weekend of summer."

"Everyone in town is invited," Valerie added.

"Wow. Everyone?"

"Well," Mrs. Brannon chuckled. "The town's not that big."

"That sounds like fun." Her foot sent her rocker into motion with a gentle nudge. "And a lot of work."

"Not as much work as you might think." Mrs. Brannon waved her hand through the air between them. "Everyone brings something to put on the grill, and a side dish. The boys come early to help Joe set up tables and get out the games."

Picturing the tiny population of Rockford eating burgers and potato salad on the lawn surrounding the house, Carrie couldn't help but smile. "Well, I'll look forward to it. That is," her stomach tightened, "if I'm still here."

"But it's three days from now." Mrs. Brannon's hand landed on Carrie's arm. "Surely you don't expect to leave us that soon, do you?"

"No." Her heart sank in despair. Every day that passed was one more day not knowing what was happening with her brother. But even if she knew, what could she do about it? She forced a smile. "Probably not."

"Oh, so you're not staying very long?" Valerie's expression was hard to read. "I was under the impression that you'd be here a while."

"It's still kind of up in the air."

"Morning, Valerie."

Relieved to have an excuse not to elaborate, Carrie glanced over to see Joe come from around the side of the house. Her heart did that funny fluttering thing she'd come to expect whenever he appeared, but this time it practically took flight. The sight of him ambling up the porch steps in his Levi's, muddy boots, and Stetson reignited every romantic cowboy daydream she'd ever entertained, making it difficult to think straight.

"Saw your truck." He pushed his hat back slightly, a gesture that only served to heighten his manly allure. "Figured you could use some help unloading."

Valerie had perked up at the sight of him as well. She gave him a crooked smile. "Thanks."

Jolting, Carrie remembered her plan to try to talk to someone at Lucas's work who might know how she could get hold of him. She checked her watch. It was a few minutes after eight.

"Do you mind if I use your phone to make a call? I lost mine." Afraid she'd blush if she looked Joe in the eye, she directed her question to his grandmother. "It's long distance, I'm afraid."

"Use my cell," Joe responded. "It's in the kitchen behind the cookie jar."

"Wait . . ." She frowned. "Did you say, 'behind the cookie jar'?"

He nodded, like he saw nothing unusual about that.

"See." Looking at Joe, Valerie raised a hand in Carrie's direction. "Carrie thinks that's weird too."

Joe lifted his hands in defense, a hint of humor flashing in his eyes. "Okay, one of you is bad enough. Both of you ganging up on me is flat-out unfair."

Pushing herself up from the rocker, Carrie chuckled. "Why on earth do you leave your phone behind the cookie jar?"

"Hey, if I had my way, I'd toss it in the junk drawer and let it die a slow death."

"He puts it there so he won't lose it but he doesn't have to look at it." Valerie gave him a good-natured shake of her head. "Men. Maybe you can help us train him while you're here, Carrie."

"It would be my pleasure." Catching Joe's eye, it hit her how that had sounded. "I mean . . . I practically raised my brother, so I guess I'm pretty experienced at training men." She swallowed her rising mortification. "I should go make that call."

Dipping her chin, she beat a hasty retreat into the house, hoping that no one had noticed the pink in her cheeks or the quiver in her voice.

Chapter 12

Joe noticed Valerie keeping a keen gaze on Carrie as she disappeared into the house. The moment the screen door shut, she turned to him with a too-bright smile and a curious glint in her eye.

"Carrie seems nice." In spite of the smile, her voice sounded pinched. "Where's she from?"

"We don't know, exactly." Grandma's tone held more than just her customary concern.

"Oh?" Valerie folded her arms, a little too interested for Joe's liking.

"She had some trouble with her car." He hoped that would be enough to quell her curiosity.

"That's awful."

"She got stuck in Rockford waiting for Hal to get a new tire." Grandma added in an obvious failure to intercept Joe's telepathic message that they should change the subject. "It's going to take a few more days. She needed a place to stay, so we offered."

"You mean, she's a stranger?" Valerie's voice lowered as she took a couple of steps closer to them. "You don't really know her?"

Joe bristled at the implied accusation in her tone. "We do now." Sure, he sounded defensive, but he didn't like where this conversation was headed. Or rather, what it was carefully skating around. Why did he feel like he had done something wrong that actually needed defending?

"Okay. So ..." Valerie frowned and tipped her head to one side, clearly putting too much thought into what he *wasn't* telling her. "... she's staying here. And she's helping out around the ranch while she waits."

"She needs to make some money." With a wave of her hand, Grandma invited Valerie to sit in the chair Carrie had vacated. "Poor thing is going through some kind of trouble."

As she lowered herself into the rocker, Valerie glanced at Joe, clearly hoping he'd fill in the gaps.

"We don't know any more than that." Not exactly true, but he wasn't about to go spreading Carrie's personal business around. Especially not to Valerie, who seemed a bit too emotionally invested in this situation, making it all the more complicated.

"We know she's running away from something." From anyone but Grandma, that would have sounded like gossip, but the pure caring in her heart came out in her voice. "We just don't know what it is."

Joe rubbed his forehead. This was one can of worms he hadn't wanted to open in the first place, and now that they had, he wanted to herd those worms right back in. He gestured to Valerie that they should get to unloading her truck, but she ignored him.

"She's on the run?"

"Yes," Grandma answered. "And since she needs money, I thought we should offer to let her stay a while and work for me."

"Well." Valerie sat back, pushing the rocker into motion with her foot. "It's obvious what's going on here."

Joe's hackles went up. Sure, this conversation was long-overdue. But this wasn't the time. He needed to change the subject, and fast. "Look, I—"

"A woman doesn't just take off with no money unless she's getting out of an abusive situation. And that cut on her face? She's obviously running from a violent boyfriend, or maybe a husband."

Joe flinched. That wasn't what he had expected her to say. Not even close. *An abusive relationship? Maybe . . .*

Grandma nodded. "That would make sense." She looked at Joe. "Dear, why didn't we consider that possibility?"

Joe gave them both a long blink. This was none of their business, and he really didn't want to include Valerie, of all people, in their speculating.

After working his jaw for a moment, he jabbed his thumb in the direction of the driveway. "Why don't you move your truck around back. I'll be there in a minute to help unload."

Valerie hesitated then stood, the disappointment on her face painfully apparent.

As soon as she'd stepped out of earshot, Grandma started in on him. "You need to make up your mind one way or the other about that girl. It's not fair to allow her to keep her hopes up."

Joe closed his eyes and let the air slowly vacate his lungs. Guilt plagued him. Grandma was right. He'd left Valerie hanging for too long. Not wanting to commit, but not quite willing to let go either.

The sad thing was, she was a great person. Always had been. And when it came to women in this town, she was pretty much the only one he'd ever even considered settling down with. But there was something missing. Something he'd seen between both his parents and his grandparents. And from the stories they had filled his head with his whole life, that thing had been there for them from the start.

Sure, it could grow with time. But was it too much to expect that he might meet someone he could feel that way about at first sight? Kind of what he felt when he thought about—

"—Carrie. The poor dear." Grandma *tsked*. "I'm surprised at us for not considering that possibility."

He snapped out of his contemplation, realizing that he'd missed a hunk of what Grandma had just said. "What possibility?"

Her look flashed irritation at his inattentiveness. "That she's escaping an abusive relationship. It happens all the time." She took in an abrupt gulp of air. "You don't suppose that was the man who was in her motel room, do you?"

"I don't know." Joe shrugged. "Could be. That would make about as much sense as anything." Only, why not just admit that? And why not get the police involved?

She didn't wear a ring . . . he'd happened to notice that detail. But that didn't mean she wasn't married. His stomach started to burn. The stories he'd heard about men who got abusive, even to the point of violence, with the women they were supposed to love and protect were enough to make his blood boil. A fresh surge of protectiveness for this woman he barely knew flooded through him.

Enough. He didn't want to dwell on the possibility that she might be a battered woman. Strange as it seemed, he'd almost prefer finding out that she'd committed a crime. In a weird way, it would be easier to stomach than knowing she'd been a victim of abuse by someone she'd trusted.

"She'll confide in us in due time." With a decisive nod, Grandma sat up straight. "Once we've won her trust. Women who have been beaten—"

"Let's not leap to any conclusions." Lowering his voice, Joe took the once-again unoccupied seat. "We still don't know what her story is. We might not ever know. She could be running from the law."

"Now, if she were some kind of criminal, do you think she would have told you she thought she killed somebody?"

"I don't know. Maybe. I don't know how criminals think."

"I don't believe she's a criminal. You've always said I'm a good judge of people. And I think God directed her path to you, Joseph Henry Moder."

He drew back. There was no arguing with Grandma when she hauled out his full name. Not to mention that her saying his middle name, the one that had been given to him to honor Grandpa, always served as a subtle reminder that she expected him to live up to her high expectations. To be the man of honor that Grandpa had always been. It was a lot to live up to.

Shaking his head, he stood and strode back around the side of the house, wishing this problem would just disappear.

Chapter 13

After easily finding Joe's phone, Carrie retreated upstairs, relieved that she could make her call in private. She'd been nervous that either Joe or his grandmother might overhear something. Now, she could speak freely.

Once in her room, she bumped the door shut and quickly found the On button. The screen came to life and, thank goodness, didn't demand a password. She swiped away an image of a mountain range, revealing an open text conversation with someone named Jeremy. Before she even realized what she was doing, she had read the most recent message.

> *Saw you walking into the diner. She's a babe!*

Her stomach clenched as she quickly hit the Home screen. She really hadn't meant to snoop.

But . . .

Who was Jeremy, and who was this "babe" he was talking about? A pang of irrational jealousy pinched at her nerves.

Wait . . .. What was she thinking? The jealousy swiftly gave way to a blend of flattery and embarrassment as she realized that Jeremy, whoever he was, had probably meant *her*.

That must have been the text Joe had received while they'd been sitting together. The one that had made him smile. The notion that he might have told his friend about her brought a rush of warmth to her cheeks.

She shook it off. This was no time to be acting like a high school girl with a crush on the unattainable star of the football team. She had to stop getting so distracted.

And besides, she wasn't the only "babe" on the block. Valerie was obviously a frequent visitor to the ranch and, unless Carrie missed her guess, she'd like to make that situation more permanent.

Pulling her thoughts together, she made a quick call to her office, happy that no one ever answered the main line so she could just leave a message.

"I had a family emergency. I needed to leave town in a hurry . . ."

True.

". . . then, wouldn't you know, I lost my phone."

Also true.

Her boss wouldn't care. As long as she closed deals, which she regularly did, he didn't ask for the day-to-day details.

On the verge of starting to ramble, she ended that call, then tried to recollect the name of the place where Lucas had been working for the past couple of months. She pondered. It was a company that installed entertainment systems in people's houses. How many of those could there be in Seattle?

A quick search turned up a surprisingly long list, but one toward the top rang a bell. Absolute Power Audio Video. That sounded right.

She hit the phone icon and let out a long breath as it rang.

"APAV." The brusque voice of a middle-aged male came on the line. "Can I help you?"

She felt suddenly underprepared. His manner, along with the indistinct sounds of a busy workplace gave the impression that she had called at an inconvenient time. Should she say who she was? Or just get to the point?

"Is Lucas there?"

"Lucas?"

A note of apprehension in the word made her stomach tighten. Had she called the wrong place?

Then he added, "You mean Yost?"

"Yes. Lucas Yost." She closed her eyes. One step closer. "Is he there?"

"No." His voice got quieter, and the background noise faded as if he'd stepped into a private office. "He isn't."

Her heart sank, along with her hope that whatever had set off this chain of events had blown over and Lucas's life had returned to normal.

"C-can I leave a message for him?"

"You can leave a message, but I don't guarantee he'll get it." The man let out a soft breath. "Do you . . . know him well?"

The question caught her off guard. Why would he ask her that?

"I'm his sister." She hesitated before asking, "Is something wrong?"

"His *sister*." His upward inflection on that word made her think he was pleased by her answer. "Carrie. Isn't that right?"

Lucas talked about her at work? That didn't seem like him, but it was nice to know.

"Yes." The tightness in her throat that she assumed she'd moved past returned. "And . . . I'm sorry . . . you are . . . ?"

"I'm Bob. Lucas's boss. I'm glad you called, Carrie."

Bob. She remembered now. Lucas had told her about his boss when he'd first started this job. How he liked to act as a mentor to the young guys he hired to install the equipment. At the time, she'd been preoccupied with her own work, and if she were honest, tired of hearing about every new promising aspect of Lucas's life that would eventually lead to nothing.

Now, the details trickled back to her in a flood of gratitude. This man had taken her adult orphan of a brother under his wing. Why hadn't she at least acknowledged the significance of that?

She cleared her throat in an effort to regain her composure. "Lucas has told me how much he enjoys working for you."

"Good to hear." He made a sound like he was sucking in air, perhaps choosing his words carefully. "But frankly, I've been concerned."

A sickening feeling washed through her. Lucas had a history of messing things up for himself. A string of jobs which he'd either quit or been fired from. But this one had seemed different. He'd told Carrie he'd finally found something he enjoyed that he thought he could stick with. But now . . . Was this just another instance of immature recklessness? Or something more serious?

"Concerned." She swallowed. "Why?"

"I hate to say this, but he hasn't shown up for work all week. Do you have any idea where he might be?"

Her heart sank. Of course, it shouldn't surprise her that he'd vanished without contacting his boss. Knowing him, it hadn't even crossed his mind to do the responsible thing. But Bob was like a father figure. He'd said it himself. Why hadn't he at least given him a call?

"No." The frustration that always accompanied any discussion of Lucas's behavior with someone else who was affected by it settled in. "I was actually hoping you might know."

"I wish I did. He hasn't been answering his phone."

"He can't. He doesn't have it."

"Oh? Did he lose it?"

"Sort of." This was so complicated, and she really didn't want to get into those details. "You know Lucas."

A soft chortle told her that he did. "I've had a feeling he might be in some kind of trouble. When he applied for this job, his résumé showed a sort of . . . colorful work history."

"Colorful? You mean, lots of low-paying jobs he didn't stick with for long?"

Another chuckle. "Exactly. To be honest, this business attracts a lot of young men like Lucas. I pay real well and train them on the job. I like to give people a chance to prove themselves."

"That's very kind of you."

"Thank you. But the fact is, some of them prove themselves to be lazy dishonest bums. I had higher hopes for your brother." He held a beat, then added, "Still do."

"Yeah, I do too." She leaned back against the pillows on her bed, taking comfort in the opportunity to talk to another person who understood Lucas. This was a rare occurrence. "I'm afraid he might have done something stupid." Hard as that was to admit, it felt good to confide in someone she could trust. She was sick of being in this alone.

"Well, you know him better than I do. But let's not assume the worst. He's got a good head on his shoulders."

Her hand went to her mouth as she felt a sob well in her throat. She was so used to being on the defensive when it came to her brother. This was the first time in years that someone had given her an encouraging word about him.

She tried to speak, but all that came out was a raspy little, "You're right."

"Does he have any close friends?" A tapping sound started in the background, like he was consulting something on his computer. "Anyone he would go to?"

"I don't really know any of his friends. He talks about Zander—"

"Of course. Zander. Anyone else?"

"I've racked my brain. Maybe if you ask Zander, he could tell you who Lucas hangs out with."

"We've talked. He can't think of anyone. I'm looking at Lucas's résumé now. What about this job he had in Idaho? In . . . what town was that?"

"A little place called Burton."

"Burton . . . Idaho." More tapping. "Yes. Did he make any friends there?"

"Not that he talked about. He was there for such a short time before he . . ." She let that thought rest. That job had ended with a shouting match over commissions, if she remembered the story correctly.

"You both came up from California, right?"

"That's right. Sacramento. We have an aunt still there, but . . . we haven't spoken to her in years. And I know he hasn't kept in touch with anyone from school."

"You never know. Believe me, I've seen these guys get into some pretty big messes. And more often than not, they want to run back home."

Home. The sound of the word made her throat tighten. Neither of them had had a real home since Mom and Dad died.

"Well, thanks for your help, Bob. Please let me know if you hear from him. I guess you can see the number I called from. That's the best way to reach me for the time being."

"It sounds like your life might be in transition too right now."

"You could say that."

"Try not to worry, Carrie."

She bit her lip. Something about the way he said her name felt paternal and comforting. She shouldn't have belittled her brother's need to find someone to replace Dad. Maybe she could use a father figure herself.

After blubbering out an emotional end to the call, she sat quietly for a moment. Bob was right. She had to trust that this wasn't as bad as she'd feared.

Chapter 14

That afternoon, having learned how to operate the decades-old but still functioning washer and dryer, Carrie left Mrs. Brannon sorting and folding in the basement to go deliver the clean towels.

Feeling heartsick and helpless, she had rolled over all her options in her mind. The only thing that kept her from calling the police to report Lucas as missing was his warning not to involve the authorities. At the time, she had dismissed his declaration that his life would be in danger if the police got involved as histrionics, but she didn't want to take the chance.

It seemed like her best option was to proceed with her plan to help Mrs. Brannon while she waited for her car. Then she could return to Seattle and search for Lucas herself. He was pretty much all she had in the world. What else was she supposed to do?

On her way up to the second floor, she paused on the landing to look out the small leaded glass window. Joe was working in one of the fields, looking like something out of a tourist brochure for the state of Montana. Realizing that she was staring, she jolted herself out of it and continued up the stairs. What was with her, anyway? She hadn't been so distracted by a man since she'd had that slight crush on a coworker at the real estate firm she worked for.

Her stomach buckled. *Worked.* That could very well be past tense if she didn't get this mess sorted out soon. If too much time passed, she'd have no choice but to leave another message. But what would she tell them? *I'm hiding from someone who tried to kill me and wants to get to my brother, but please don't call the police?*

After adding the clean towels to the cabinet in the upstairs bathroom, she was about to head back downstairs when curiosity struck. This was such a large house, but she'd only seen a few rooms. Now that she looked around, it hit her how elegant the place was. It was like something you'd see in a magazine or a TV show featuring well-maintained historical homes.

Taking advantage of the quiet moment, she moved past the bathroom, peering through the open door to one bedroom, then another. Both looked similar to the room she occupied, comfortable but not personalized. Joe had been right when he'd said they had plenty of room for guests here.

There was one more door, this one closed, right at

the end of the hallway. Could that be Joe's room?

She contemplated taking a look, but thought better of it. No point in being too nosy.

Although she had to admit, she really wasn't as interested in the house as in the people ... or one person in particular ... who lived in it.

With a sigh, she headed back toward the stairs. She took a step down, then glanced over at the cute seating area adjacent to her. She paused, one foot hovering over the next step down.

Tilting her head, she saw that there was another door just past the large bookcase. She reversed her direction, then took a couple of careful steps. Just enough to allow her to see through the doorway.

Something about this room set it apart from the others. It looked masculine. Lived in. She moved closer.

It was Joe's room.

A tingle of guilt arm wrestled with the thrill of getting an inside look into Joe's personal space. This was it. The epicenter of his universe. The room he'd probably had since he'd come to live with his grandparents as a child.

She knew it was wrong to spy, but he had left the door open. She wasn't seeing anything that wouldn't be visible to anyone who wanted to grab a book and cozy up in one of these antique armchairs.

She stood there, a couple of feet from the threshold, not daring to breach an unspoken trust. But drinking in every detail, nonetheless.

A window on the far wall looked to be the same as the one in her room, but with a view of the fields behind the house and the mountain range beyond. There was a wooden rocking chair next to a small bookcase. She strained but couldn't see any of the titles. From this angle, she could see one end of a dark wood footboard. Easing a couple of steps to her left, she angled for a better view. A masculine-looking quilt in shades of blue and beige draped the mattress, and she chuckled at the observation that it was slightly askew. So, he was a man who made his bed. A little imperfectly, but that only proved he was human.

Something on the table next to the bed caught her eye and she squinted to see if it was what it appeared to be. *Yes.* A Bible. Not positioned for display, but with one corner hanging over the edge of the table like he'd set it aside as he'd shut off the light for the night.

A flash of guilt washed over her at her own neglect of her once-rich spiritual life. She used to keep her Bible on her bedside table too. Sometimes, she'd even fallen asleep with it next to her on the bed. But those days were long gone.

She had only been to church a handful of times since moving to Seattle, something she had blamed on a failure to find a church that met her needs. But, deep down, she knew that was just an excuse. The fact was, since losing her parents, she'd been harboring a grudge against God.

Tears pressed against her eyes and she blinked in a futile attempt to keep them from falling. Why was emotion overwhelming her now? After all these years, wasn't she about cried out?

Suddenly weak, she leaned forward, allowing the

doorframe to support her weight. What was wrong with her? Yes, she missed her parents and grieved the unfair way they'd been taken from her. And the pain of knowing that Lucas was in trouble and there was nothing she could do to help him weighed on her. But there was something else weighing on her. Something she couldn't quite—

An ear-splitting *crash* jolted her upright. For a long moment, she felt disoriented. Then she flew into motion. As she hurried toward the staircase, she had a terrible feeling of foreboding. Hitting the landing, she stopped cold.

To her horror, Mrs. Brannon lay facedown at the bottom of the stairs.

Chapter 15

While he'd been tempted all day to make some excuse to pop into the house to see how things were going, Joe had held out till his stomach told him it was nearly time for dinner. When he walked into the kitchen, he was met with the familiar sight of a woman in front of the stove, her back to him. But it wasn't the woman he'd grown accustomed to seeing there.

It was Carrie. Looking right at home.

Smiling to himself, he cleared his throat. "Don't tell me you convinced her to put her feet up while you get dinner?"

She jolted, whipping around like her mind had been a million miles away.

"Whoa. Sorry." Holding his hands up, he took a step back. "I guess I need to make a little more noise when I come in the house."

"No, it's . . . I'm just jumpy. It's not your fault."

He tipped a sideways nod, then crossed to the sink to wash up. The smell of something savory wafted his way and he took a glance at the big pot she'd been tending to on the stove. "Dinner smells great. Don't tell me that's vegan?"

A nervous titter sputtered out as she reached into the cupboard for some bowls. "It's vegetable soup. But don't worry. I found some pork chops in the freezer, so I'm baking them. And I'm warming up some bread. No one will go hungry."

"Including you, I hope." He reached for a towel. "Guess we need to get to the store to stock up on . . . what is it you eat, anyway? Chickpeas? Tofu?"

Taking the bowls to the table, she tossed him a tentative glance. "You don't need to worry about me."

Drying his hands, he studied her as she set the table. Her shoulders looked so tight they practically reached her ears. And her hands were shaking. Could she really be that unsure of her cooking . . . or was something else making her tense?

He looked around. "So, should I tell Grandma it's ready? I'm assuming you had to tie her hands together to keep her from helping you cook."

"That's not far from the truth."

The sound of Grandma's voice brought his head around. He gasped. There she stood at the end of the hall leading to her bedroom, looking sassy as ever, with her right arm in a sling.

He threw Carrie a questioning glare, which she deflected by looking away.

His heart pounding, he turned back to Grandma. "What is going on?" Reaching out, he took a step toward her.

"Now, don't you make any fuss." Entering the room, she batted him away with her good hand. "It isn't broken."

"How do you know?"

"I've been living with this arm for over seventy years." She crossed to the oven and flicked on the light to check its contents. "I think I'd know if it was broken. Besides, Carrie knows first aid." Her eyes lit up as she peered through the smudged window. "Oh, those chops look just perfect. I'll get us some applesauce." She disappeared into the pantry.

"First aid?" He turned on Carrie. "She's not a kid with a scraped knee."

"I know that. Look, don't blame me. I wanted to call 9-1-1 and she said it would take a couple of hours for an ambulance to get out here."

"Why didn't you ring the bell? I would have come."

"She wouldn't let me. She said she just needed to rest."

"And you believed her?"

"She just twisted her wrist. It doesn't look broken."

Letting out a long breath, he rubbed at the growing tension in his forehead. "Exactly how did this happen?"

She stopped, leaning a hand on the back of a chair. "She fell. On the stairs. See, she was in the basement, and—"

"She fell coming up from the basement?" This had been one of his biggest fears. Why hadn't he moved that blasted washing machine up to the main level of the house?

"No, no. The main stairs. I was up there putting away towels, and—"

"So why was she going up the stairs? You're supposed to be watching her."

"Oh, for pity's sake, Joseph." Grandma appeared in the pantry doorway, a jar of applesauce braced against her abdomen. "Don't blame Carrie for this. It was my own clumsiness."

His jaw worked. He really didn't care what Grandma said. Carrie was supposed to be preventing bad things from happening, not facilitating them. "I'm taking you into town tomorrow to see the doc. You hear?"

"The doc has better things to do than to tell me what I already know. That I need to rest and take plenty of Tylenol. There. I just saved us a hundred-dollar office visit."

"Grandma, I—"

"You're making too big a deal of this." She set the jar on the counter. "Now, I'm going to go freshen up for the lovely meal that Carrie has prepared for us. When I return, I expect the subject to be closed." She turned on her heel and ambled toward the back bathroom.

Willing his pulse to slow before he spoke again, he lifted his gaze to Carrie. Her expression had turned dark, like her nervousness had morphed into self-defense.

"Honestly, Joe. I think she's fine." She crossed to the counter and picked up the jar of sauce. "I've seen a broken arm or two in my day, and I really don't think it's that bad."

"That's not your call to make."

"You're right." Her attempt to open the jar seemed to frustrate her further. "I'm sorry. But I don't think it's fair for you to blame me here. Your grandma told me not to call and, in case you hadn't noticed, she's very strong-willed."

He grabbed the jar from her and unsealed it with one smooth twist. "If you're going to be here with my grandmother, I need to know that I can trust you."

"Trust me? What if I hadn't been here? Who would you be yelling at right now? Am I just here so you have someone to blame whenever anything goes wrong?"

Her face reddening, she ran out of the room.

Joe just stood there, feeling completely helpless. All he knew was that Grandma had gotten hurt and he hadn't been able to prevent it. He had failed her. And he had no clue how he was supposed to deal with that.

Chapter 16

Pulling the front of the sweater she'd borrowed from Mrs. Brannon tighter around her neck to stave off the brisk morning air, Carrie stepped out onto the front porch. She scanned the drive, barely seeing half as far as normal, thanks to the rain that had turned torrential a half hour or so ago. If this kept up, Joe might just decide to stay in town for a little while rather than risk the drive back with such poor visibility.

Letting out a sigh, she took Lucas's phone from her back pocket and perched on the edge of one of the rocking chairs. She'd blown through the list of chores Mrs. Brannon had dictated for her, and had spent the last half hour watching the local news on the small TV in the kitchen, in case anything came up about Lucas. There was nothing, of course.

She studied the phone. Even if she had the

password, what would she do? She really didn't know any of his friends well enough to determine who could be trusted, and there was a reason he had given her the phone and told her to protect it. What if she did something to tip off the wrong person that she had it in her possession?

Hugging the phone to her abdomen, she stared out at the grayness enshrouding the ranch. As if things weren't bad enough, now she felt responsible for Mrs. Brannon's injury. Of course, she wasn't directly responsible, but if she had just gone back downstairs after delivering the towels instead of pandering to her curiosity about Joe, it wouldn't have happened. And how could she think of leaving now that Mrs. Brannon literally needed her to act as her right-hand woman?

Feeling the effects of her restless night, she twisted her head from side to side. But when she did, a movement over near the barn caught her eye. Stomach plummeting, she slowly stood. Was it just the rain? Maybe a tree moving in the wind. Some kind of animal?

Or . . . something more sinister.

Her heart raced. Why had she thought it was a good idea to stay here alone instead of accompanying Joe and his grandmother to the doctor? If that man found her here, she'd be a sitting duck. No car. No means of escape.

That thought propelled her into action. She darted back into the house and shut the double doors, then twisted the lock, which seemed an ineffective barrier against someone who was truly determined to get to her.

What about the back door? Her heart leaped to her throat. Joe had come in that way for breakfast and, knowing what she did of his habits, he hadn't even thought of locking it.

She moved through the house like her life depended on it. Once in the mud room, she twisted that lock too as she pressed her nose against the cold glass of the window in the door. She couldn't see anyone, but that did little to reassure her. He had found her once. And now, she had convinced herself that he was out there.

Watching.

Waiting for just the right moment.

Taking in air in short gasps, she hurried back into the kitchen. As she checked the view of the barn from the kitchen window, she tried to collect her thoughts. Did this house have any more doors? If they made a habit of leaving their doors unlocked, would they be any more vigilant with the windows? She'd have to go room by room, checking every entry.

Then she remembered . . .

The basement.

Basement windows were notoriously neglected. Broken. Left unlocked. Wouldn't that be the first place someone would try to break in?

She turned to face the basement door, which had, up until this moment, seemed like any other door. Only now, it felt ominous. Like the gateway to her doom. She couldn't go down there to secure the windows. No way. And of course, that door had no lock.

Thinking fast, she dragged a kitchen chair and propped it under the knob. It was a feeble effort at best, but at least if anyone tried to come up from the basement, they wouldn't be able to do so silently.

She stood there, her eyes fixed on the makeshift barricade, almost certain that her pursuer had already broken in and was going to burst through at any moment.

An abrupt pounding noise from somewhere behind her yanked her around with a shriek. Fresh panic welled in her stomach.

But through the window, she saw Joe's truck in the driveway. He was home! And the pounding suddenly made sense.

Feeling foolish now for being so afraid, she hurried into the entryway. Through the cut-glass windows in the front doors, she saw Joe shaking an umbrella and his grandmother hunched under the hood of a too-big rain slicker.

Carrie unlocked the doors and pulled one open. "I'm sorry. I locked it."

"Yeah, so I see." Still sounding a little surly, Joe guided his grandmother in. He set the umbrella down on the bench by the door as he closed it behind them.

"You don't carry a house key?" Carrie reached out to help Mrs. Brannon with the slicker, which she now saw was draped over her thin shoulders. Her right arm, while in a fresh sling, also sported a wrist-to-elbow cast.

"It's on the keys I keep in the truck."

Carrie bristled. "You mean, even when you lock the doors, your key is right outside for anyone to—"

"Now, stop bickering, you two." Mrs. Brannon smoothed her hair with her good hand. "Carrie's right. Go out and get your keys."

"Fine." Growling out a breath, Joe shook his head and opened the door. "I need to bring in the supplies I got anyway." With that, he exited back out into the rain.

Carrie looked at the cast. "Did the doctor say it was broken?"

"He said it's a slight fracture." She batted her other hand as if that might lessen the impact of her words. "Just a thin crack."

"So it *is* broken." The weight of this situation hit her fresh. "No wonder Joe still looks mad."

"He'll get over it. It's really not a big deal."

"But . . . you should be sitting down." Carrie hated how jittery her voice sounded. "Why don't I make you a cup of tea while you take a load off.?"

"*Take a load off?*" She balked. "Between you and that overprotective grandson of mine . . ." Her scoff turned to a reassuring smile. "The last thing I need is to be treated like I'm incapable. But, having said that, a cup of tea does sound good."

The front door whooshed open again to Joe, now completely soaked, holding a lidless cardboard box.

"Don't think you're taking that to the kitchen without removing those muddy boots first." After scolding Joe, Mrs. Brannon patted Carrie's arm. "I'll be waiting in the kitchen." She winked. "'Taking a load off' my wrist."

Setting the box on the bench by the door, Joe watched his grandmother amble out of the room.

"So it's a fracture. You were right." Carrie wrapped her arms around her midsection. When he didn't respond, she shifted her focus. "What's in the box?"

"While Grandma was waiting at the pharmacy, I picked up a few things to keep you from starvation."

She peered in to see tofu, a jar of almond butter, and several different kinds of beans. "That was thoughtful of you."

He nodded slightly. "You mind taking it to the kitchen? Day's half gone and I need to get back to work." He turned, reaching for the door.

"In this rain?"

"Rain or shine ..." Raising a brow, he almost smiled. ". . . work still needs doing."

"Yes, I suppose. Oh, hey ... wait ..." She jolted, remembering her fear from earlier. "You said you sometimes hire people."

"Yeah?" He paused, the door half open.

"I was just wondering if you had anybody right now. Working here, I mean."

"Got Mike coming in tomorrow to do some fence work. Rest of my summer crew starts next week. Why?"

"No reason. I just thought I should know what to expect."

Nodding slowly, he studied her for a few seconds before taking his leave.

She stood there, watching through the windows as he darted across the yard and into the barn.

Her fear from just a few minutes ago seemed a little ridiculous now. She hadn't actually seen a person. Not for sure, anyway. Still, as she picked up the box and headed for the kitchen, an uneasy feeling settled in the pit of her stomach. That man had gotten to her so easily before. What would prevent him from doing it again?

Chapter 17

By the time Carrie entered the kitchen, Mrs. Brannon had the kettle on the stove and two flowery china cups with a basket of assorted teas set out on the table.

"I thought you were resting." Readjusting her grip on the box of vegan supplies, Carrie watched Mrs. Brannon move about her kitchen like she'd been kept in confinement too long.

"I'm fine." In spite of her perpetual motion, she seemed a bit more low-key than usual; probably a result of either the pain or whatever the doctor had given her to subdue it. "I'm making tea for the both of us."

"You're a terrible patient." Carrie felt her face droop. "And I'm a terrible helper. What good am I if I can't even prevent an emergency?"

"It wasn't an emergency, and what do you think

you should do? Follow me around with a net?"

"No, but—"

"Besides, the doctor gave me a lesson on how to catch myself, in case it ever happens again. It was very informative."

"Just don't get any ideas about running away to become a stunt woman." Carrie dipped a nod at the box. "Mind if I put this away?"

"Go ahead, dear. There's plenty of room in the pantry."

A moment later, Carrie stood in the nice-sized storage space, scanning the colorful rows of canned goods that looked almost more decorative than utilitarian.

"There should be a box of shortbread cookies in there," Mrs. Brannon called out from behind her. "Unless Joe got into them. That boy does have a sweet tooth."

"I've noticed." She quickly found space on a lower shelf to hold her goods, then, with shortbread cookies in hand, returned to the kitchen.

"I see you've redecorated." Pouring water into the cups, Mrs. Brannon tipped an amused glance at the basement door. "But that might be impractical for sitting."

"Oh, right." Carrie quickly placed the cookies on a plate, then took it and the barricade chair with her to the table. "I got a little nervous being here all alone. It's silly, I know."

"Not in the least, after all you've been through." As they both took their seats, Mrs. Brannon's brow crinkled. "So, that man in your motel room. You believe he's still after you?"

Heat burned Carrie's cheeks. The last thing she wanted was for Mrs. Brannon to fear for her own safety.

"I don't think so." She flipped through the colorful bags of tea, pretending to consider her choices. "I'm sure I scared him off."

"Oh? How did you do that?"

"Well, I . . . stabbed him. At least, I think I did."

"You did?" Her blue-gray eyes flew open so wide, they mimicked the cornflower saucer under her cup. "You're a hero. Good for you." Smiling, she gave Carrie's hand a firm pat.

Surprised by the show of support for her desperate act of self-preservation, Carrie braced herself for a barrage of questions. But Mrs. Brannon just hummed a little as she picked out a bag of tea, then tried to open it with her one good hand.

"Let me help you with that." She reached for the bag, but Mrs. Brannon wrenched it away.

"Carrie, dear. I have to get used to this. I'm going to be living with this cast for a couple of months and you've said yourself you don't know how long you'll be here."

"But you're paying me to help you."

"You can help me by letting me work out how to do the simple tasks. When I really need help, I'll let you know."

As painful as it was to watch, Carrie just sat there as Mrs. Brannon held her packet between the bent fingers of her injured hand and tore it with her good hand. She winced a little.

Carrie winced too. "Did that hurt?"

"It's no worse than my arthritis. I guess that's why this doesn't seem like such a big deal to me. And besides—" She dipped the bag in her cup. "—the Lord will see me through."

Carrie nodded, absentmindedly taking a teabag for herself. "It's good that you believe that."

"Don't you?"

"I used to. The truth is ... both of my parents died of cancer when I was eighteen—"

"Oh, dear. I'm so sorry to hear that."

She nodded, blinking back tears. "And my trust in God died right along with them. That sounds terrible, doesn't it?"

"Lots of people turn their back on God when something like that happens."

"You think so?"

"I know so. When my daughter and her husband were killed, I went through the very same thing."

"You did?"

Sadness filled her eyes as she slowly nodded. "It was an incredibly dark time. I truly questioned if God even existed."

Carrie leaned forward. "What did you do?"

"I forced myself to get out of bed every morning." Pursing her lips together, she looked out the window, her gaze growing distant with the far-off memory. "We had Joe to raise, and things still needed doing around here. But to be honest, that first year I was just going through the motions. Everything in me went numb, including my faith in God."

Carrie felt a jolt of sorrow shoot through her like

an arrow. Her own grief and diminished faith had leveled out to something that she had come to think of as her new normal. The possibility of coming out of this tunnel into a restored belief in God hadn't really occurred to her. She needed to know more.

"So," she swirled the teabag in her cup, "how did you get it back?"

"It took time. And I had my Henry. We were able to support each other. And good friends who showed me God's love through their kindnesses." Mrs. Brannon's hand shook as she lifted her cup, as if keeping it steady in her non-dominant hand presented a challenge. "And there was Joe, of course. Sometimes the blessings aren't so easy to see, but they're always there."

"I suppose that's true."

"We had a lot of good years." She blinked, her eyes growing liquid. "Then I lost my husband."

"Did you blame God for that?"

"Not 'blame,' really. But I admit to feeling angry at God for leaving me here to go on without Henry. I've been praying to get past it, but sometimes I still feel ..." She rolled her hand in front of herself, searching for the right word.

"Stuck?" Carrie offered.

"Yes. Stuck. That's the word. Like quicksand." Mrs. Brannon looked like she might want to ask something, but held back. Instead, she gave her a sympathetic smile. "You and I are both stuck, aren't we?"

Carrie lowered her eyes, nodding slightly. She *was* stuck. In more ways than she cared to admit.

"We both need to find a way to move on." Mrs. Brannon tapped the table like she was making a declaration. "I'll add you to my prayer list."

"Thanks. I appreciate that." And she meant it, knowing Mrs. Brannon was good for her word, whether or not Carrie believed the prayer had the power to help her. Raising her cup to her lips, she paused, then added. "Would you mind praying for my brother too? He's been even more lost than me. And now . . ." She paused again, not wanting to admit that he might be lost in a very literal sense. "Now I'm not really sure what's going on with him."

"I certainly will. What's his name?"

"Lucas." She smiled lightly, staving off her emotions.

"Lucas," Mrs. Brannon repeated.

As Carrie sipped the soothing tea, she actually felt better, even though nothing had changed. Oddly, she felt like some of her burden had been lifted.

Chapter 18

Carrie bolted upright, gasping for air, certain she was about to die.

Catching her breath, she looked around the room. There was no man holding a pillow over her face. No one lurking in the shadows. She was safe.

She dropped her face into her hands. All she wanted was to rest so she could think clearly tomorrow. But the storm churning outside her window had no doubt contributed to her dream-haunted sleep.

That, along with the two cups of tea she'd had before bed . . .

As much as she detested the prospect of crawling out from under the comfy covers, there was no point in trying to fall back asleep until she used the bathroom.

Stepping into the hall, she quickly checked to see that Joe's door was shut. The thought of waking him up was unnerving, especially now that she seemed to have secured a spot on his enemy list.

Well, maybe *enemy* was a bit strong, but she'd certainly lost points with him for failing to adequately handle his grandmother's injury. And maybe he was right. Maybe she should have listened to her gut instead of to Mrs. Brannon. She understood now that acting as caregiver was part of her job, even if that hadn't been clearly stated to her.

A few minutes later, she exited the bathroom and shut off the light. She was about to head back to her room when a loud *bang* stopped her cold. She stood stock still, listening. But all she heard now was the howling of the wind.

Then it came again. *Bang*.

Adrenaline coursed through her like water in a spring thaw. The sound had come from one of the three rooms toward the front of the house. She crept carefully past the two dark rooms she could see into, hearing nothing but the pounding of the rain against the windows. Slowly, she moved toward that mysterious closed door at the end of the hall. She leaned forward until her ear was just an inch or so from the door.

Bang.

With her heart in her throat, she whirled around and collided with a wall of solid flesh. She ricocheted backward, slamming into the door. Her eyes focused on the dark form.

"Whoa, there."

Joe.

She heaved out a breath. "You just about gave me a heart attack."

"Oh, really?" Stepping forward, his features grew clear enough for her to see that he seemed amused. "Lucky for me you didn't have your pocketknife on you."

"Oh, you're a comedian now." She pushed herself away from the door in an attempt to regain her balance, if not her dignity. "Why are you skulking around in the middle of the night?"

"*Skulking?*" One side of his mouth lifted as he reached around her and opened the door. He flicked a switch, illuminating a small overhead light, then headed straight for a large bay window directly across from the door.

Carrie followed, but stopped in the doorway, her gaze sweeping the room. At about twice the size of the other bedrooms, this was clearly the nicest one in the house. By the items set out on the bedside tables and the dresser, it was easy to figure who had last occupied it.

"How long has it been?"

"Since what?" His brow creased as he tossed her a look.

"Since your grandpa passed."

He opened one of the side windows and reached out to latch a shutter that had clearly been striking the glass. Whatever lightheartedness he'd felt a few minutes ago appeared to have fallen away. "Sorry about the noise." He shut and locked the window. "I need to replace that latch one of these days."

As she watched him move silently toward her, seeming to avoid her gaze, she assumed he either hadn't heard her question or was choosing not to answer it.

Way to put your foot in it, Carrie.

She was about to step out of the room when he answered.

"Yeah . . . I guess it's been about six years now."

"Oh." She looked up at him, surprised at the emotion choking his voice. "I assumed it had been more recent. I mean, I know it's none of my business, but . . ." She looked around the room at the items that seemed to be waiting for their owner's return. "Have you considered packing up his things? Maybe donating to other people who might be able to use some of them?"

He looked at her, his forehead scrunching like this was a totally foreign idea.

"I'm sorry." Leary of losing whatever ground she'd just regained in their tenuous relationship, she quickly backtracked. "It's really not my place to . . . It's just that your grandmother told me she feels stuck. Maybe this is part of the problem."

"It's not just her." Casting his eyes downward, he ran a hand through his sleep-tousled hair. "Neither of us has been able to face it. Too many memories."

"Maybe I can help. I mean, sometimes it takes an outsider to make decisions like this. Lucas and I . . ." She stopped, swallowing hard.

His head snapped up, and he finally met her eyes.

Realizing how little he actually knew about her, she quickly filled in that gap. "That's my brother.

There was no way we could have dealt with our parents' stuff by ourselves. I was eighteen and he was only fourteen."

"You were just kids."

"Yeah." And if she hadn't gotten legal custody of him, he would have become a ward of the state. Would things have gone any better for him if he'd been taken in by another family?

Shaking off that thought, she continued. "I had a friend who came over right away and helped us."

Amy. They used to be best friends, but Carrie hadn't so much as thought about her in years. Had she even told her how much she'd appreciated her support back then?

"Anyway, it really helped us to get on with our lives. Maybe it would help your grandmother too. And you."

"Yeah." He seemed unconvinced. "Maybe one of these days." He turned off the light and held up a hand as if to invite her back out into the hallway. As they moved silently toward their own rooms, Carrie chided herself for being so forward. Obviously, she'd crossed a line.

Chapter 19

Wiping her brow with the back of her hand, Carrie waited as Mrs. Brannon took a bite of warm apple pie.

"Well?" Carrie scrunched her face in anticipation. "What do you think?"

"Mmmm." Mrs. Brannon chewed slowly, her expression remaining neutral. But as she swallowed, she broke into an encouraging smile. "No one would ever guess that this is your first pie. It's delicious."

"Thank goodness." Carrie released a breath. "I wouldn't want 'the boys' to be disappointed."

Mrs. Brannon had told her all about the crew of young men who worked for Joe during the summer months. For most of them, their return for the season would be at the barbecue on Saturday, and they all swore they'd keep taking the work as long as there was pie.

"They'll be happy to know that someone else around here knows how to bake." Mrs. Brannon seemed to catch herself. "That is . . . for now."

"It helps to have a good teacher." Carrie looked at the unbaked pies—three regular and one vegan—waiting to take their turn in the oven. "Thanks for teaching me."

"It's my pleasure. My daughter, Mary, used to love watching me bake. She was such a good student too. Got to be that she was better at it than I was."

"I doubt that's true." Carrie opened the oven and placed two of the pies on the rack, then shut the door and set the timer. "Things always taste better when someone else makes them, don't you think?"

"Too true. I'm awfully glad you were here to help. I have to admit that one-handed pie baking is a little beyond me."

"I think it would be beyond most people." Carrie smiled at her as she wiped the excess flour from the counter into her palm. "I can see figuring out the rolling pin, but how would you peel and slice all those apples?"

"Reminds me of that movie. The one where the girl lost an arm to a shark."

"You mean, Bethany Hamilton?"

"Yes. She didn't let a little thing like a shark attack stop her from living."

Carrie chuckled. "Let's just be grateful you were climbing the stairs and not surfing. *Your* arm will recover."

"Praise Jesus." She yawned. "Speaking of 'recovering,' I think I'll lie down for a bit. The doctor wasn't kidding when he said these pain killers would make me sleepy."

"You rest. I've got everything out here under control."

Mrs. Brannon gave her a soft smile and shuffled down the hallway to her room.

Once the last pie was in the oven and well on its way to golden perfection, Carrie poured herself a glass of iced tea and, taking the timer with her, went out to the back porch. Finally, after twenty-four hours of ark-worthy rainfall, the day had turned warm and sunny.

The encouraging song of an unseen bird soothed her soul as she sat down on an inviting wicker chair and took a sip of tea. Under different circumstances, she could totally get used to this.

As things stood, the best she could hope for was some temporary ease from her stressful situation while she waited for word that her car was ready.

A movement out in the field caught her eye, and she strained to see a figure near the fence. His arm pulled back and he took a swing. Must be the guy Joe had mentioned that he had coming to do some fence work.

Just as she was getting cozy, Joe came out of a shed some distance from the house carrying a shovel. Seeing her, he tipped a nod.

She returned the greeting, her heart kicking it up a notch. He'd been quieter than usual at breakfast, but at least he didn't seem to be holding a grudge against her anymore. Trying to ignore him, she let her gaze wander to the peaceful fields and the mountain range beyond. When she saw from the corner of her eye that he had propped the shovel against the shed and was headed her way, her heart kicked it up another notch. Make that two notches.

Great. He could probably hear it.

"Pie smells good." He ambled up the steps, stopping at the top and leaning against the post like he had no idea how disarmingly rugged that made him look.

"I'm glad I was here to help." Taking a sip of tea, she did her best to appear relaxed, as if his presence didn't make that next to impossible. "We even made a vegan version."

"Vegan pie?" He cocked his head, looking off in the distance like he was trying to picture such a thing. "Sounds . . . interesting."

She chuckled. "I bet you wouldn't even notice the difference."

"I'm pretty much a pie aficionado, in case you didn't know."

"An *aficionado*, huh? That's a ten-dollar word."

His jaw twitched. "From a two-dollar rancher?"

"That's not what I meant." Did he really think she was a snob just because she lived in a city? *Was* she? Best to let it drop. "I'm not quite sure what to do with myself now. Your grandma says we're ready for the barbecue. And she's taking a nap."

"Good. Because I was thinking you might want to go somewhere." He chewed his lip, like he wasn't quite confident about what he wanted to say. "Get out of the house and enjoy a little sunshine."

"Don't you have work to do?"

"There'll always be work to do. Come on." He tipped his head away from the house, like a kid trying to convince a pal to play hooky with him. "We wouldn't be gone long. And Mike's out back, in case Grandma needs anything."

Her stomach tingled as she studied him. It had been so long since she'd been asked out by a man, she didn't even know what to think. Not that he was asking her on an actual date or anything, but still.

She was about to answer when a buzzing noise made her jump.

Huffing out a laugh, she reached for the timer she'd set on the table next to her. "My last pie is ready to come out of the oven, so ..." She gave him a resigned smile. "I guess I have no excuse."

Chapter 20

When Joe had suggested they "go somewhere," Carrie had no idea he'd meant "on horseback." So when, an hour later, she found herself in a saddle on a dainty brown horse named Posey, she felt like a real city slicker.

Joe looked over his shoulder, obviously much more at ease than she was. "You okay back there?"

"I'm fine." Her voice sounded high and jittery, partly from nerves and partly because of the way Posey jostled her as she clopped along the uneven trail.

"We're just about there," he called back, a touch of amusement evident in his voice.

"Great." She couldn't help but wonder what kind of teasing she was in for tomorrow when she found walking a challenge. Still, she had to admit that it felt good to get some fresh air, and the scenery was magnificent.

Her eyes gravitated to the "magnificent scenery" on the back of that big black horse leading the way. A sly smile snuck onto her lips. This whole nature trail thing had its unexpected benefits, no doubt about that.

As the horses clip-clopped along, the afternoon sun flickered between limbs of the trees on either side of them. Birds sang in a soothing chorus that, if they continued riding much further, might just lull Carrie into forgetting her problems.

But before that could happen, they rounded a bend and the trail opened up to a clearing. In front of them, a burbling river ran between them and the mountain range, which was still quite a distance away but almost looked close enough to touch.

"Oh ..." Carrie gasped as Posey stopped next to Joe's horse, clearly privy to the protocol. "It's so beautiful."

"Not a better sight in the whole world, you ask me."

She watched as he de-horsed—or whatever that process was called—wanting to ask how much of that world he'd actually seen, but afraid he might take that the wrong way.

He tied the reins to a low-hanging tree branch, then stepped over to help Carrie dismount. Once she'd regained the feeling in her legs, she moved a little closer to the water and sat down on a fallen tree trunk.

Joe came along beside her, and took a seat on the

other end.

She gave him a sideways glance, hoping to size up his demeanor. "You come here much?"

"Not enough. Usually when I need to feel closer to the Lord."

That shouldn't surprise her, considering that he'd been raised by Mrs. Brannon, and no doubt shared her beliefs. "So you come here to pray."

"Or just to feel the quiet." He picked up a rock and flicked it across the water. "I thought this might do us both good. It's been a rough week."

"Yeah." Suddenly antsy, she looked from one side of her to the other. A momentary panic caught her in its grip. She liked Joe, but how well did she really know him? "Where's your house from here? I'm feeling a little lost."

"Over that way just about a mile." He pushed his cowboy hat back from his forehead and dipped a nod to the left. "Not as far as it seems."

"Oh. And, you're sure Mike will hear the bell if Mrs. Brannon—"

"I asked him to check in on her. He's done it many a time when I've been out with the cattle. Or gone into town." He frowned. "We can go back, if—"

"No, no. This is nice. Let's stay a minute." She paused. "I know you worry about your grandma. I would too. But she's got a lot of pluck."

"Pluck?"

"Yes. She's not going to let a little thing like a broken bone stop her."

His almost imperceptible flinch warned her that she was treading on dangerous ground.

"I don't mean to disregard the seriousness of it. It shouldn't have happened." She took a deep breath, then added, "I'm sorry."

"I don't blame you." He tossed another rock, keeping his eyes on the water. "I'm sorry it seemed that way."

She bit her lip. It had seemed that way because it had been true, but there was no point in pressing the issue. Satisfied that at least they'd both apologized, she tipped her head back, closed her eyes, and relished the heat of the sun on her face.

"Posey took a liking to you."

When Carrie opened her eyes, she saw that Joe had seemed to relax too, leaning one arm on his thigh, and rolling a stone between his fingers.

"She did?" Carrie smiled at the vain thought that he might be projecting some of his own feelings onto the horse. This was nice, being here with him, but there was no point in thinking anything might come of it. Joe lived on a ranch in Montana, after all. And he'd probably eventually marry Valerie . . .

"You sure you've never ridden?" He yanked her from her wandering thoughts, which was probably a good thing.

"Well, I might have misrepresented my experience slightly." She picked up a stone and mimicked his tossing action, finding it unexpectedly calming. "There was this fair I went to one time. When I was about eight."

"A fair? Like, with rides and games?"

"Exactly. They had a pony ride. You know, where the little ponies go around in a circle and the kids sit on their backs. Lucas wanted to go but he was too scared, which I teased him about, naturally. But my mom asked if he'd be brave enough to do it if I did it too. He said yes. But the thing was, even though I teased him, I was scared too. But then I had to face my fear and do it."

"To prove that you weren't scared."

"Partly. But also because I knew it was the only way he would get to do this thing he really wanted to do. I've always looked out for that little monster."

"It's what you do for family."

"Yeah." Her vision got a little fuzzy as she stared off in the distance. "I got custody of him when he was fourteen. He still calls me his Carrie Mama Beary."

"'Carrie Mama Beary.'" A tiny twitch of his lips said more than his words. "I like it."

"I have no idea why I told you that. It's embarrassing."

"Hey, it beats what most brothers call their sisters."

"I guess so." She looked at him, momentarily distracted by the way the brim of his hat shadowed his eyes, adding to his still-waters-run-deep persona. "You don't have any siblings?"

"Nope. Always wished I had a brother, but I had to settle for my buddy Jeremy."

Jeremy. "Oh?" She turned away on the off chance that her face would reflect her feelings about the text she'd accidentally read. "He was your best friend?"

"Was. Still is. He's been like a brother to me my whole life."

"And, he lives in town?"

"Owns a place right on the river. Not too far from here."

"It's important to have people you care about close by." If she really believed that, why did she seem to push everybody away?

He nodded slowly in agreement. "You see your brother much?"

Her heart stumbled. "Probably not as much as I should. As soon as he turned eighteen, he moved to Seattle. I think he was trying to run from his grief, but it didn't work. And he was all alone, so I followed him there not long after."

"Running from your own grief?"

"No, I . . ." She stopped, realizing how defensive she sounded. "I guess. Maybe. Running away from lots of things. But the pain just followed me."

"Grief has a way of overtaking you when you don't just stop and let it catch up."

"That's pretty profound."

"I've done my share of grieving." His features softened, along with his voice. "I spent lots of time up here after Grandpa died. To be honest, I did a fair amount of yelling at God."

"Sounds familiar."

He slanted her a melancholy smile. "Then I realized I wasn't really mad about Him taking my grandpa. I mean, he had lived a good long life. What I was mad about was Him taking my parents."

"And that surprised you?"

"Well, yeah. I thought I was over that. But I found out the Lord had some things to work through in me. I did a lot of praying. Finally found some peace."

"I wish I could find peace." The words sounded hollow in her ears as her gaze followed the hypnotizing flow of the river. "I haven't prayed once since I stopped asking Him to heal my parents. Those prayers went unanswered, so I've been giving Him the silent treatment ever since."

"I get that."

"I wound up thinking, either there is no God or He doesn't care about me." She held an extended pause, then added softly, "I still feel that way."

"You still question if there's a God?"

"Honestly? Yes."

He nodded, more contemplative than judgmental. Not trying to convince her of His existence, or His goodness. Or of anything. Just understanding.

"And the truth is, I'm worried about my brother."

"He lost his faith too?"

"Well, yes. But it's more than just that." This was too much to bear on her own. She needed to trust him. "He's the reason I had to go into hiding."

Chapter 21

Sitting completely still for fear she'd spook like a feral horse, Joe waited for Carrie to continue.

"This all started last Sunday." She gulped, staring at her intertwining fingers. "Lucas showed up at my apartment looking like he'd had the life scared out of him. He said he couldn't tell me what was going on, but he was obviously in a hurry to get out of there." She removed something from her pocket and cradled it in her hands. "Then he gave me this."

"His phone?"

A jittery exhalation seemed to confirm that her fear was real. "He said there was something important on it that he didn't trust himself not to destroy."

That was weird. But Joe tried not to jump to conclusions. "He didn't tell you what it is?"

"No. And he was so anxious to leave, I didn't push it. I just figured this was another one of his little messes that would go away after a few days." She shook her head. "So I stuck the phone in an inside pocket of my purse and pretty much forgot about it."

"Okay." He did his best to level his voice so she'd keep talking. "Why did you have to run away?"

"The next day when I was at work, someone ransacked my apartment. I came home and . . ." Tears filled her fear-widened eyes. "It was horrible. My stuff was everywhere. Just tossed around." She flung her arm out to demonstrate. "Like they were looking for something."

"That?" He pointed to the phone.

"I guess so. I mean, what else would it be? I don't have anything to hide."

"Did you call the police?"

"I was afraid to. I thought I needed to talk to Lucas first. I didn't want to cause more trouble for him."

"*More* trouble?"

"He has a history of getting involved with the wrong people and making bad choices. Nothing illegal or anything. Just not very smart." She dropped her chin. "I've had to pull him back from the brink more than once."

"So, you talked to him instead of the police."

"Yeah. I just . . . need to protect him, so I went to his place. Maybe it was the wrong choice, I don't know. But when I told him what had happened, he freaked. He said not to call the police because they might be in on it."

"You think that's true?"

"I don't know. But some of the things he's told me about people he's known . . . You'd be amazed at the corruption."

He thought about Jeremy, and how committed he was to his job. Sad to think that not everyone in law enforcement was there for the right reasons. "People get greedy, I guess."

"Or they're just plain evil. Anyway, he told me to take his phone and get as far away as I could."

"He didn't tell you why?"

"No. And I panicked. So I got in my car and just drove. Until I couldn't go any more without sleep. Then that man found me." Her beautiful eyes widened again as she looked at him, emotion thickening her voice. "I wouldn't have stabbed him but he pushed me down on the bed and put a pillow over my face. I didn't know what else to do."

Joe couldn't help but stare at her as the weight of that sank in. But, as bad as this sounded, he felt a strange sense of relief that it wasn't an abusive partner she'd been hiding from. The urge to take her in his arms and assure her that she was safe was powerful, but he held back.

"And you s-see why I can't r-report it." Her voice came out in short gasps, like she might be on the verge of sobbing. "If anything happened to Lucas because I trusted the wrong people, I'd never forgive myself."

He nodded, pleased that she had decided she could trust him. Now more than ever, he owed it to her to do what he could to help. "Maybe if we look on the phone, we can see what—"

"It's locked." She shook her head. "And I don't know the password." She pushed a button and held up the screen to show him. "I thought about finding a tech expert, but I don't know who to trust."

"I could look at it, but . . ." His chest squeezed. When it came to fixing fences or herding cattle, he felt completely competent. Too bad that was of no use to her. "I'm not exactly good with those things."

"It's okay." A resigned sigh slipped free as she tucked the phone back into her pocket.

He pinched the bridge of his nose. "So, you think the guy who followed you to the motel was after the phone."

"That would make sense. He grabbed me when I had my own phone in my hands, which he must have taken, thinking it was Lucas's."

"Whatever's on that thing must be really important for that guy to be willing to kill for it. God was looking out for you."

"Yeah. I guess."

As they sat in silence, looking out at the water moving past them, the need to protect this woman overwhelmed him. For the first time since they'd met, he firmly believed that her story of danger was real.

He also firmly believed that, for better or worse, he was falling in love with her.

"You got a medium-rare bison burger ready to go?" Millie leaned toward the grill, a paper plate with a loaded bun on it in one hand and an icy can of root beer in the other.

Joe pressed the spatula down on one of the patties that sizzled over the fiery coals. Satisfied that the juices flowing from it were the perfect shade of pink, he slipped the spatula under the meat and lifted it to her plate. "That's what I like to see. A woman with a healthy appetite."

"Are you kidding me?" Eyeing the burger, she joined her husband, Johnny, at the condiment table next to the grill. "I'm just thrilled to have someone else feeding this bunch for a change."

Joe grinned as he checked the Kielbasas that were almost, but not quite, brown enough.

For years, come rain or shine, the first Saturday of summer had meant one thing to the people of Rockford—the barbecue at Shadow Ridge Ranch. And this year, God had blessed them with perfect weather. Hot enough for the kids to keep busy with water balloons and Super Soakers, but cool enough for the adults to comfortably relax in the shade.

Joe let his gaze travel around the backyard, which was teeming with activity. Kids chased each other on the grass while adults clustered around the long tables, filling their plates with fresh fruit, baked beans, and every kind of salad known to man. Under the shade trees, card tables and folding chairs had been set up for eating and socializing. Which people seemed to be doing with gusto.

He was about to return to his cooking when something else caught his attention. Carrie, whom he'd hardly seen all day, stood at the bottom of the back steps, looking radiant. Sunlight glinted off her loosely swept-up blond hair, giving her an almost otherworldly radiance. She wore a flowery sleeveless sundress that he thought looked familiar but couldn't quite place. She hadn't borrowed it from Grandma, that was for sure.

He stared. Mesmerized. She was, without question, the most beautiful woman he had ever seen.

But when it came to knowing how to help her, he was at a complete loss.

"Hey, Joey. What's that in your eye?"

Joe lurched at the abrupt realization that Jeremy had appeared next to him and he hadn't even noticed. "What are you talking about?" He snapped his focus back down to the burgers. "I don't have anything in my eye."

"I think they call it a 'glint.'" Jeremy held a metal spatula an inch from Joe's nose. "Look for yourself."

Joe swayed sideways, batting away the spatula with a good-natured swat. "Get that thing out of my face."

Jeremy complied. "So, when am I going to meet her?"

Joe grabbed a set of tongs and poked at a Kielbasa. "Who?"

"Who." Jeremy picked up a large plate and held it over the grill. "The girl behind the glint."

Joe didn't want to admit to anyone, not even Jeremy, that his feelings for Carrie were intensifying.

That just wasn't very smart, especially considering how much he still didn't know about her.

"You'll meet her. Don't worry. Just—" He pointed the tongs at Jeremy's chest. "—don't ask her anything personal."

"What do you think I'm going to ask? Age? Weight? Social security number?" His tone turned serious. "What else have you found out about her, anyway?"

Joe turned away, still undecided about how much more he should share with his friend. While he hadn't exactly made any promises to Carrie, if he told Jeremy too much, he knew she would see it as a betrayal.

"I got a few details." He carefully removed the cooked meat to the plate. "But if I tell you, I need you to swear you'll keep it under your hat for now."

"You do know that hat is issued to me as an officer of the law, right?"

"I know. How about if you take *that* hat off for a minute and put on your fishing hat instead."

"Because you're making me fish for information?"

Joe chuckled. "Exactly right." Joe gave Jeremy a condensed version of what Carrie had told him the day before.

"That's some story. You believe her?"

"No reason not to." Joe waited until a couple of teenagers had grabbed some hotdogs and moved on. "I think we should just drop it for now, all right?"

As he added more burger patties to the grill, Joe looked over at the shady area under the big mountain-ash tree, where a gaggle of church ladies encircled Carrie like a swarm of bees in a flower garden. He snickered to himself. Maybe she shouldn't have worn that floral print.

By the way she stood there, all stiff and not really looking anyone in the eye, Joe guessed that she wasn't thrilled about being the center of attention. But she didn't need to worry. Knowing this group of ladies, they were trying to sell the new girl in town on their single sons or grandsons. Even if she *wanted* to talk about herself, she'd have a hard time getting a word in.

"I called around." Jeremy wasn't heeding Joe's request to drop it. "Nobody showed up in any hospital anywhere in the state that night with a stab wound. If she really did go after some guy with a knife, she couldn't have hurt him too bad."

"That's good."

"Yeah. Except if he didn't get what he wanted from her, he's probably even more determined. I don't want anybody to get hurt."

"I don't want that either."

"Look, I understand why she might not trust the police, but if what she said is true, she needs protection."

"If?" Joe tossed him a look. "Why would she invent a story like that?"

Carrie turned just then and their gazes intertwined. She tossed him a pained wince that he read as a plea for help.

Jeremy shrugged. "Could be to cover up a crime she committed."

"Hold on." Joe turned his full attention to his friend. "You said you checked her history and she's clean."

"I said *Carrie Yost* is clean. Did you ever stop to think she might have assumed a fake identity?"

Shaking his head, Joe focused on the grill. "You watch too many crime shows."

"Hey, I have to do something to keep my skills honed. Is it my fault we don't have any real crime in this town?"

"Careful what you wish for, my friend." He handed him the spatula. "Man the grill for me, will you?"

"Where are you going?"

"I need to rescue my houseguest from her starring role on this week's episode of *The Bachelorette*."

Chapter 22

"His name is Birch." The little gray-haired lady who'd introduced herself as Betty had wasted no time telling Carrie all about her grandson, and explaining why he had reached the age of forty-two and never married. "He even owns his own home."

"It's a cabin in the woods," a woman named Margaret—or was it Marion?—snapped.

"That he built himself." Betty glared defensively at her cohort.

"With no electricity or indoor plumbing." Another woman, Doris, chimed in. "Or heat."

"There's a woodstove." Betty corrected her friend, then put her hand on Carrie's arm. "I really think you'd like him, dear. I'll let you know the next time he comes into town for supplies."

"Ha. Bullets and beer." Margaret-or-Marion grumbled. "*Those* are his supplies."

The other ladies concurred as Betty scoffed.

"Afternoon, ladies."

Carrie whipped around, thankful beyond words to see Joe approaching the group. The women eyed him with suspicion and closed ranks around Carrie like she was Beyoncé and they were her entourage.

She held back a laugh. Apparently, Mountain Man Birch and his ilk couldn't hold a candle to Handsome Rancher Joe.

"I hope you're all enjoying yourselves." The perfect host flashed a model-like grin as he reached in to extract Carrie from their ranks.

She stepped out into the sun, feeling like she'd been rescued from a shark tank.

"If you'll excuse us." He tipped a nod at the women and led Carrie by the elbow toward the safety of the side yard.

As they walked, she let out a breath. "I get the feeling there aren't a lot of single women in this town."

"Sad, but true." He glanced down, like her comment might have touched a nerve. Then he switched gears. "You look real nice."

"Oh, thanks. I realized I didn't have any party clothes, so your grandma asked Valerie to bring something."

"Ah, yeah." He nodded. "I thought that dress looked familiar."

Not quite sure how to take that, she ducked under the shade of a sprawling tree and took a seat on a rustic wooden bench she found there. "So, this is it, huh?" She kicked off her—or rather, Valerie's—flip flops and surveyed the scene in front of them. "The entire population of Rockford?"

"Give or take." Sitting next to her, he scanned the crowd. "You already know some people." He gestured with his chin. "Valerie. Millie. That's Millie's husband, Johnny. He cooks at the diner."

As he continued down the short list of people she might find familiar, she let her gaze wander.

The area between the house and the barn had filled up early in the day with the cars of the first arrivals, leaving everyone else to park along the side of the road leading up to it. At the end of the line-up, a rusty old sedan had just pulled in. A man got out and stood there, resting his arms on the top of his car and perusing the crowd like he was there to find someone rather than join the party.

Her breath caught.

It was that guy she'd seen the other day in the drugstore.

Apparently noticing he didn't have her attention, Joe stopped talking and tracked her gaze.

"Huh." For a man of few words, he could pack a barnful of meaning in a single syllable.

She squinted, trying to get a clearer look. "Who is he?"

"Name's Gil. Works for Hal over at the auto shop."

"I see." Relieved to hear he was someone Joe knew, she relaxed a little. "Must be why he drives that nice *vintage* car."

"Yeah, he's a real class act." His voice sounded dark, like there was more behind his comment than just a subtle dig. "Don't get me wrong, he's good with cars. But on a personal level, he's a rat. I don't trust him."

"Why not?"

"He worked for my grandpa one summer. Let's just say, it didn't go well. I'm kind of surprised he's here, to tell you the truth."

"Really. What did he—"

"Well, look at that." Joe's focus shifted, and his expression lightened.

Carrie turned to see another car come over the rise of the long driveway. It slowed, then eased in behind the sedan.

"My car!" She leaped to her feet, clapping her hands like her horse had just taken the lead in the Kentucky Derby.

Joe stood too. "Guess that explains it."

"Explains—?" But he had already taken a couple of strides toward the driveway. She bent to retrieve the flip flops and scurried to keep up.

"Hey, Hal." As they approached her car several moments later, Joe reached out to shake the hand of the man who'd gotten out of the driver's seat. "This is Carrie."

She admired her brand-new tire. "Thanks a lot for fixing my car."

"My pleasure. I hope you don't mind that I drove her out here." Hal handed her the key fob, then reached into the backseat and brought out a box containing several bags of chips. "Thought I'd save you going into town, since I was coming here today anyhow."

"No, I don't mind." She couldn't stop smiling. "In fact, I'm thrilled. What do I owe you?"

"Oh . . . uh . . ."

Hal frowned, then looked to Joe, who gestured him toward the house.

"Why don't you go on and grab a bison burger before they're all gone."

Looking like he'd dodged some kind of bullet, Hal started up the drive. Gil joined him, seeming a little less than thrilled about being there.

Joe watched the two of them for a second. "Hal probably talked Gil into coming so he'd have a ride back to town. That's the only—"

"Did you pay for my tire?" Folding her arms, Carrie cocked her head to try to catch his eye.

He huffed out a long breath. "It was just easier to have him put it on my tab." He shifted on his feet, probably bracing himself for her to argue with him.

But her anger at what on the surface seemed like an act of charity melted into gratitude. How could she stay mad at him when he'd done so much for her?

"Fine." She actually laughed. "But you'll take it out of my pay."

"Good enough." He angled his head toward the house. "We should go. I left Jeremy in charge of the grill, and I think I smell something burning."

Chapter 23

After eating more than her fill of salads and vegan pie, participating in a water balloon fight, and coming in third in the annual horseshoes tournament, Carrie sat at a picnic table with Joe and a bunch of his friends, feeling like she'd known these people for years.

"I'm telling you . . ." Kelsey, who was a little older than Joe and married to a rancher named Tom, licked barbecue sauce off her fingers. "The best thing about eating outside is that I don't have to sweep the floor afterward."

"I know what you mean." Candace, who looked like she'd barely cleared high school but already had three kids, stood next to the table bouncing a baby on her hip. "After a meal at our house, the *pigpen* looks clean compared to my kitchen."

Laughing, Carrie glanced across the table at Joe, who seemed to fit in just as well with his married friends as his single ones. This wasn't like in the city, where there was a distinct social dividing line. Single men there had limited tolerance for talk of diapers and domesticity. To these guys, it seemed perfectly normal.

Catching her eye, Joe winked.

She quickly dropped her gaze, her heart melting faster than the ice in her lemonade.

A muffled ringtone drew everyone's attention to Jeremy, who was seated next to Carrie. He reached into the pocket of the denim jacket he'd draped across the bench between them. His face turned serious as he checked the screen.

"'Scuse me a minute." He stood and walked away from the table.

"That man never stops working." Kelsey rolled her eyes.

Valerie nodded. "I guess it's good he's still single."

Carrie marveled at that. Jeremy was a good-looking guy, just like Joe. And Valerie could pass for a model. They were all fun, intelligent people. Apparently, it wasn't just city singles who had a hard time finding a mate.

"Well, I don't know about you all," Valerie swung her legs over the bench and stood. "But I'm going to see if there are any of those pecan bars left."

"I'll go with you." Cal, who had been engaging in an entirely one-sided flirtation with Valerie all evening, jumped to his feet to follow her.

Carrie suppressed a wince. He was a decent-looking guy but the fact that he had spent the evening bragging about himself like he was God's gift to women had pretty much killed whatever sympathy she might have had for him.

She swirled her glass of lemonade and pulled the cardigan Valerie had warned her she'd need once the sun started to go down tighter around herself. Her original plan had been to help Mrs. Brannon as much as she could until the party kicked into gear, then beat a surreptitious retreat to her room. But before she knew it, she was enjoying herself so much she forgot to leave.

Now, as she listened to the ongoing banter around her and marveled at the vibrant colors of the setting sun, it occurred to her that she hadn't had this much fun in a very long time.

The teenage DJ started an upbeat song that sounded a little bit country and a little bit rockabilly. A *whoop* went up from the crowd.

"I love this song!" Candace twirled around like the baby on her hip was Fred to her Ginger. "I have to find my hubby so we can dance."

In the next few moments, there was a mass exodus as people made their way to the big clearing that had become a makeshift dance floor. They formed several lines and started kicking up their heels in a clearly choreographed routine, like real life had suddenly morphed into a movie musical.

When the dust cleared, Carrie saw that she and Joe were the only ones left at their table.

He let out a laugh. "I haven't heard this song in years."

"How does everybody know what to do?"

"It's a line dance. Pretty much a requirement for every wedding reception, prom, and family reunion in the state of Montana."

"I see. Well, considering that I have two left feet, I guess it's a good thing I live in Washington."

"City girl doesn't dance." Joe's eyes glinted playfully. "Good to know."

Carrie tapped her foot in time to the music, noting that even some of the kids were joining in. She was about to say that maybe it wouldn't be so bad if they stood in the back, when Valerie ran up to their table and grabbed Joe by the arm.

"Come on. I need you to dance with me."

Joe's eyebrows shot up. "Why?"

"If Cal gets me out on the dance floor, he'll try to keep me there till they play a slow song. And you know how he is." Looking at Carrie, she stage-whispered. "All hands."

Letting out a little laugh, Joe looked at Carrie. "You mind?"

"Of course not."

Of course, she *did* mind, but how could she admit it? He had a moral obligation to save Valerie from Mr. All Hands.

As Valerie pulled Joe over to join the crowd, Carrie slumped down with her chin in her palms, feeling like the only wallflower at the ball. As hard as she tried to keep her eyes off Joe and Valerie, she couldn't help it. They moved in perfect sync, like they'd done this dance together a hundred times.

As they spun around, the skirt of Valerie's just-above-the-knees denim-blue dress flared out, revealing well-toned legs. Her skinny belt was the same shade of rosy brown as her short cowgirl boots. She had to know how adorable she looked. And how well she coordinated with Joe in his jeans, western shirt, and cowboy boots.

She glanced down at her own outfit, seeing it in a different light. Even though it was closer to a style she would have picked for herself, she had to wonder if Valerie had been intentional in her wardrobe choice for each of them—making *herself* look like the one who belonged on Joe's arm.

She immediately retracted the thought. Valerie had been nice enough to loan her a dress, and it was really pretty. It wasn't fair to question her motives. Besides, Carrie was the infiltrator here, not Valerie. Who could blame a girl for defending her territory, consciously or otherwise?

Vaguely aware of someone approaching the bench next to her, she turned to see Jeremy shoving his phone into the pocket of his jacket. He tossed it back onto the bench between them as he swung his leg over to take a seat.

"Everything okay?" She dipped her head toward the phone. "That call looked serious."

"Oh. Yeah." He shrugged. "Technically, I get the weekends off. But sometimes it doesn't work out that way."

The reminder of her own unauthorized *vacation* made her chest tighten. "What do you do?"

He smiled a little, like there was something funny or ironic about the answer to that question. "I'm . . . uh . . . in security."

She nodded, wondering what exactly needed securing in a town the size of Rockford. She was about to ask, when he beat her to the punch.

"So, Seattle, huh?" He took a swig from the bottle of root beer he'd left sitting on the table. "What do you do there?"

Hesitating only slightly, she tried to sound confident. "Real estate. Commercial, mostly." She looked away, hoping he'd take that as a sign that she didn't want to elaborate.

"Fascinating line of work." Jeremy tapped the table in time to the music. "Must be a big change for you. Working on a ranch."

Her stomach tightened. Why was he so interested in her? Not that he shouldn't be, of course. Her situation was . . . fascinating.

"I really appreciate the opportunity." Acid burned her throat. What was she going to do if his questions turned more probing? She had to do something to end the conversation. Her mouth moved ahead of her brain, and she blurted out, "Want to dance?"

His eyebrows went up, then he seemed to consider the offer. "All right."

She heaved out a sigh as they both stood. At least looking like a fool on the dance floor beat looking like she had something to hide.

Chapter 24

Surprised by how well he remembered the steps, Joe hooked his thumbs in his front pockets and turned to the right along with the rest of the group. But as they started the next sequence, something at the far end of their line distracted him. Were his eyes playing tricks on him, or was that Carrie?

He did the next turn, but his head stayed put as he tried to get a better look. Sure enough, Carrie and Jeremy had joined the fun.

So, City Girl might have a little country girl in her after all. The thought gave him a ray of irrational hope.

Curious to see how she was doing, he stole another look. Her smile was as wide as the big night sky. And as far as the footwork went, she was actually doing pretty well.

He chuckled.

For a tenderfoot.

The song ended, and Joe joined in with everyone else, clapping and hollering. It had been eons since he'd stopped working long enough to have this kind of fun. Too bad it hadn't been alongside the woman who made taking a break from work seem worthwhile.

"Thanks for the dance." Valerie put her hand to her throat like she was trying to catch her breath.

"My pleasure." He gave her a little bow, like some kind of British gentleman.

As the next song started up—a predictably slow one—people around them either paired off or returned to whatever they'd been doing before. Joe looked over to where Jeremy was clearly asking Carrie if she wanted to dance again, but she shook her head. He smiled to himself as they headed back to their table.

Of course, he didn't want to leave them alone for too long. Being the sheriff, Jeremy was apt to get inquisitive if the opportunity presented itself. The last thing Joe wanted was for Sheriff Hingson to say something that might tip Carrie off to the fact that Joe had repeated her story without her knowledge.

"Joe."

Snapping out of his thoughts, he realized that Valerie had been trying to get his attention. He looked over to see her standing there with her arms wrapped protectively around herself, her blue eyes brimming with a hope he'd let linger there for too many years.

"I said," her voice was airy and a little breathless. "Do you want to dance again?"

He looked down, his hand moving to the back of his neck. Valerie made a sound so soft it was almost imperceptible. When he looked at her again, the hope had vanished.

Dropping her chin, she blinked like she might start to cry. "It's not ever going to happen with us, is it?"

His stomach fell. What was wrong with him? Valerie was a good friend, and he genuinely liked her. The thing was—for no reason he could put into words—he just didn't see himself ever *loving* her.

Time to man up and face this.

Dodging the dancing couples, he pulled her to the sidelines. He took in a deep breath and looked her in the eye. "You deserve so much better than—"

"Don't." She held up a hand, tears pooling as she looked away.

So this was what it felt like to be the lowest snake on earth. Why had he been so selfish? Tossing her just enough crumbs to keep her around in case he decided she was the best he was going to find. That was completely unfair.

"I've known." She swallowed hard, obviously not wanting to break down in front of people. "For I don't even know how long. But I just kept hoping." The last words came out on a little sob.

He stared at the ground near their feet, painfully aware of the slow love song and the couples all around them swaying in time to it. He wanted to kick himself.

"We should get back to the table." Valerie swiped at her eyes, giving him a forced smile. "The ice in my lemonade is melting. And it looks like Jeremy might be making a move on your girl."

He squinted at her. What had she just said? As she started to walk away, he scrambled for a response that wouldn't sound idiotic.

Seeing that he hadn't budged, she rolled her eyes and retraced her steps back to him. "Come on, Joe." She let out an unsteady laugh. "Anybody can see you're both infatuated."

What? He started to deny it, but the word "both" had rendered him speechless.

"Just do yourself a favor." She seemed to buoy herself as she continued. "Don't string her along. Remember, she doesn't live here in Rockford." Jabbing a finger at his chest, she pinned him with a squinty-eyed glare. "So you'd better give her a reason to stay."

She abruptly pivoted around and continued on toward the table, leaving him floundering at her unexpected command disguised as advice. How thickheaded was he that he needed the woman whose heart he had just broken to keep him from blowing it with the woman he loved?

When they joined Carrie and Jeremy at the table, Valerie seemed to have regained her composure.

"I think Cal's coming this way." Wringing her hands, Valerie cast a quick look over her shoulder. "I might still be in danger."

Joe glanced back, confirming that Cal wasn't in pursuit. In fact, the last time he'd seen him, he'd been kicking up his heels with Loni and Patrice Hogan, the only girls naive enough to be impressed with his big-man-on-the-ranch braggadocio. If Joe had to make a guess, he'd say Valerie was in the clear.

"Jeremy, come on." Valerie gestured with her head toward the dance area. "It's your turn to be a hero."

Having just taken his seat, Jeremy let out a grunt. "It's always my turn to be a hero. It's what I do."

Chuckling, Valerie waved him on. "Well, come on, Man of Steel. Let's dance."

As the two of them headed for the dance floor, Joe retook his seat across from Carrie, right back where they'd been just a few minutes before.

Nothing had changed, yet everything was different.

He let out a nervous chuckle, suddenly feeling like an awkward teenager at his first dance. "Now, that wasn't so bad, was it?"

"No." Maybe it was just the endorphin rush, but her smile seemed brighter, like maybe something had shifted for her too. "In fact, I think I caught on pretty well."

"It's not as hard as it looks. Next time, you'll feel right at home."

"Next time, huh? Is there a barn dance every Saturday night in this town?"

"Never thought of throwing a dance in the barn. The horses might not like it."

"Well then. If there's going to be a 'next time,' I guess it has to be tonight."

He studied her, his stomach tying itself in a knot. "You saying you're up for another dance?"

"I might be."

"Well then." He stood and gave another little bow. "Let's go."

She rose, then looked down like something had fallen off the bench next to her. As she bent to pick it up, her smile dropped and her brow furrowed. He leaned forward. Jeremy's denim jacket lay on the ground.

Carrie stood, staring at something she had just picked up.

Joe's stomach dropped.

It was Jeremy's wallet, open to reveal his badge.

"Your best friend is the sheriff?" She looked up at him, her face a study in confusion. "Why didn't you tell me?"

Her question left him at a loss. Why *hadn't* he told her? It would have made things so much simpler.

When he didn't answer, a fire ignited in her eyes. "He told me he was in 'security.' It makes sense now."

"Carrie, listen—"

"He knew I live in Seattle. He asked me about my job. He was trying to get me to talk." She shot him an accusatory glare. "What did you tell him about me?"

Joe looked around, running a hand through his hair. He knew that talking to Jeremy had been the right thing to do, so why did he feel like a louse?

He drew in a breath. "I asked him to run a check on your plates. Just to make sure that everything was okay."

She glared at him. "After I told you not to call the sheriff?"

"But . . . you didn't explain why."

Her look grew dazed like she was recalling that night they'd first met. "I don't believe this." She took a couple of steps back then turned and charged toward the house.

Great. He moved as quickly as he could around the table in an effort to catch up to her, dodging some kids playing a game of tag and almost tripping over Mr. Myerson as he slowly passed by carrying two large pieces of cake.

By the time he reached her, she was on her way up the back steps. "Carrie, hang on. Let's talk about this."

At the top of the steps, she stopped, turning, but not quite looking at him. "Fine." She folded her arms and waited for him to speak.

Letting out a breath, he checked to make sure that no one was within earshot. "I'm sorry I didn't tell you, but can you blame me? You said you thought you had killed someone. I had no idea what was going on."

"So how much did you tell him?"

He closed his eyes, not wanting to admit this to her, but knowing he couldn't lie. "Everything."

Her eyebrows arched. "Everything? You told him about Lucas and the phone?"

"You don't have to worry about Jeremy. He's one of the good guys."

"That's not the point. I explained to you that Lucas has gotten involved with shady people in the past. If someone who has a vendetta against him has an alliance with some corrupt police officer, it doesn't matter how good everybody else is. If Jeremy put any kind of feelers out about this, my brother's life could be in danger. Don't you understand that?"

"I'm sorry. I—"

"I can't believe I trusted you."

She took a step back, and he moved to follow her.

"Don't." She held up a hand, firing another angry glare. "I can't talk to you right now."

She hurried into the house, leaving him feeling like he'd just had the wind knocked out of him.

Chapter 25

It was almost midnight, and Carrie hadn't slept a wink. She'd been too keyed up to do anything but cry, pace, and peer out the window at the departing guests.

From what she could tell by her partial view of the parking area, most of them had filtered out shortly after she'd fled to her room. She'd braced herself for the inevitable check on her welfare from either Joe or his grandmother, but it never came. Now, since it was late and she'd turned out her light, she suspected they were giving her space until morning.

She reversed her path across the braided rug next to the bed. What was she going to do? She still had no idea where Lucas was or what she could do to help him. And now . . . now that she knew she couldn't trust Joe . . .

A strange little tune cut into her thoughts. At first, she assumed it was the DJ starting up a fresh round of dance music. But it was too close. Coming from inside her room . . .

Wait. Was it . . .?

Lucas's phone!

Frantic, she dove for her purse on the bed and yanked at the zipper. She had no idea who would be calling him, but whoever it was might have some idea of his whereabouts. Or be able to get a message to him.

Snagging the phone from the inner pocket, she willed it to keep ringing long enough for her answer. Her hand trembled so much, she could barely hit Accept.

"Hello!" Her breath held in her throat as she waited for a response.

Silence. Then a hesitant voice. "Carrie?"

Relief tumbled out in a shaky little laugh. "Lucas!" Tears instantly filled her eyes. "Where are you? Tell me what's happening."

"Why haven't you been answering your phone?"

Her jaw clenched. If she told him about the man in her motel room, that would lead to more questions. She had to get answers from him first. "I lost it. I wanted to call you, but—"

"You don't have your phone? Man!"

"It's okay. I have this one."

"No." The sharpness in his voice alarmed her. "You can't use that phone. I should have warned you to keep it turned off."

Instinctively, she glanced at the device in her hand like it was a ticking timebomb, then returned it gingerly to her ear. "Why?"

"Because he might be able to trace its location."

A fire lit in her stomach. "*Who* might?"

"Here's what you need to do." The urgency in his voice rose. "Go get a burner phone."

"A what?"

"It's a disposable phone. Then call me on that. I'll tell you this number, but I need you to just remember it, okay? Don't write it down."

"O . . . kay." Not trusting her scrambled brain to remember her own name much less a phone number, she reached for the pen and notepad she kept in her purse. She scribbled as he fired out the digits.

"Got it." She shoved the notepad back into her purse. "Is the phone you're on safe?"

"Don't worry about that. Just call me as soon as you can. Turn my phone off and hide it real good. Don't lose it, whatever you do." He paused. "It might be the only thing that keeps us alive."

Terror, along with a million unasked questions, coursed through her. She sputtered out a heart-wrenching goodbye, then held down the Off button on his phone. As the screen snapped to black, her body went numb.

The sounds of cheerful conversation outside drew her back to the window. She peered out through the opening in the curtains, hoping to remain unseen. A small crowd of Joe's friends—it looked like the young singles were closing down the party—laughed and talked as they made their way to the center of the parking area. They lingered for a moment, then dispersed to their various vehicles. Joe shook Jeremy's hand—she could only imagine how their conversation had gone after she'd left—and Jeremy got into a truck. The only remaining vehicle, aside from her own car of course, was the Hayes Family Farm truck.

No real surprise there.

Joe turned and disappeared from her view. For probably a full minute, she stood there waiting for him to escort Valerie to her truck. But neither of them appeared.

So . . . she was still here.

A fresh sense of betrayal surged through her as she pictured the two of them, cozying up in the front room or sitting on the front porch. It was irrational, she knew. But Joe had acted like he was interested in *her*. What was he trying to do? Keep both of them on the line?

No. She didn't need these confused emotions clouding her thinking right now. He had already shown her he couldn't be trusted with her secrets. It wasn't much of a stretch to see that he couldn't be trusted with her heart either.

Moving from the window, she made a new plan. One that would get her away from here.

To Joe's way of thinking, the only problem with having their annual barbecue on a Saturday was that Sunday morning came way too early.

A yawn inflated his chest as he filled Posey's trough and gave her a good-girl pat on the flank. Leaving her stall, he rolled his head from side to side. Another hour in bed sure would have been nice.

Of course, all his friends who didn't have kids to get home had stayed long after good sense had called it a night. It had been fun, but the situation with Carrie had definitely killed his party buzz. And his strong suspicion that Valerie had wanted to talk things out before she left hadn't exactly helped. By the time they had the chance, Carrie's window had gone dark so there'd been no point in putting Valerie off. He'd done that for far too long as it was.

His head throbbed at the reminder of all the pain he'd caused her with his years of ambiguity. And it really didn't matter how many times last night he'd reassured her that she was a great person. He knew—and she knew it too—that he was saying it as much to make himself feel better as to help her through this.

There were no two ways about it. He was a heel.

As he put the feeding bucket back on the shelf, his stomach reminded him that he had just enough time for breakfast before grabbing a shower and dressing for church. But when he stepped out of the barn, something stopped him cold. His truck was right where he'd pulled it off to the side to make room for their guests yesterday. But where was Carrie's car? When he'd seen Valerie to her truck sometime after one that morning, it had been sitting all by its lonesome where Hal had left it.

He walked down the drive a ways, just to make sure she hadn't moved it. But it was nowhere to be seen. Maybe she'd been anxious to test the new tire.

Or maybe the explanation was something more worrisome.

His heart raced as he made tracks back to the house. As he entered the kitchen, Grandma glanced up from the stove.

"Would you grab the maple syrup, dear?" She flipped something on the griddle. "I'm making French toast out of those leftover hamburger buns."

Reaching for the fridge, he cast his gaze around the room in the hope of seeing something that would ease his concern. "You seen Carrie this morning?"

"Not yet. Actually, I was hoping to talk to her before you came in." She placed a golden-brown bun on a platter. "I hope she's not still upset about Jeremy."

"I hope the same thing." An uneasy feeling churned in his stomach. "But I wouldn't hold my breath on that."

Doing her best to focus on the road ahead, Carrie blinked back emotion and fatigue. This long straight stretch of highway seemed endless. If only she'd gotten an earlier start.

Since she hadn't wanted to risk slipping out while Joe was still awake, she'd been forced to wait for Valerie to leave. Getting a little shut-eye had seemed like a wise use of her time, but once her head hit the pillow, the sleep that had eluded her for hours overtook her with a vengeance. By the time she'd jolted awake, the sky had changed from midnight blue to cobalt.

So much for escaping under cover of night.

Fortunately, she'd managed to sneak out of the quiet house without alerting anyone to her plans. By the time she'd gotten into her car, the dashboard clock had read 6:25. She glanced down at it now. Only 6:50? It felt like she'd been on the road for hours.

Her plan was to put some space between her and Rockford, then find a place to buy a burner phone. But as she scanned the landscape, all she saw was narrow highway with dry grass and an occasional outcropping of rock on either side. Not so much as a gas station in sight.

She pushed the Scan button on the radio. Maybe some music would take her mind off her troubles and help her stay alert.

Static led to a garbled country song, then more static. She was about to turn the thing off when the crystal-clear voice of an older man with a charming Australian, or maybe New Zealand, accent filled the silence. She jabbed at the button to stop the scanning.

"*It is human nature to make assumptions.*"

Something about his voice seemed calming, and she actually felt her pulse slow a bit. With any luck, the reach of this station's transmission would see her through until she got closer to civilization.

"*But leaping to a conclusion can be a very serious thing. It can lead us to hurt other people and dishonor God.*"

A radio sermon. *Right.* It was Sunday. She grunted at the painful reminder that it had been a full week since this whole mess had started.

Her focus wandered in and out of the pastor's story of a personal experience he'd had. He tied it into a message about the Sermon on the Mount, and Jesus's words about judging others. As he read from the Bible, she listened with half an ear. She'd heard these passages so many times before. Back in the days when she used to study the Word and look to it for wisdom and strength. That seemed like a lifetime ago.

A mileage sign up ahead stole her attention just as her stomach rumbled a reminder of how long it had been since last night's dinner. The pain in her stomach took a sharp turn north, tightening the center of her chest.

Great. The last thing she wanted to think about right now was Joe. And how she'd been foolish enough to—

"*Why are we so quick to judge the motives and character of another person when we do not know their intentions?*"

The pastor's words sliced into her thoughts as if he were sitting in the seat next to her. Did he somehow know that she'd been guilty of judging Joe's motives without giving him the opportunity to explain himself?

She fidgeted in her seat. Now that she thought about it, the irrational notion that the pastor with the charming accent spoke directly to her might not be so farfetched. Her dad had once explained that God sometimes uses other people to deliver messages. Maybe this was one of those times.

A breath came out on a sigh. If she believed that, it meant she still believed in God. Did she? If there *was* a God and He knew she'd been unfair to Joe, wouldn't He want her to make it right?

The desire to pull a U-turn nearly won out over common sense, but the sight of some buildings up ahead snapped her back into her mission. A truck stop. What better place to buy a disposable phone.

Joe's gut response had been to get in his truck and head for Seattle, keeping his eyes peeled for Carrie's car. But by the time he made it to the highway, he'd devised a more practical plan.

Ten minutes later, he barreled into a parking spot in front of the diner, alongside Jeremy's police cruiser. Unless he missed his guess, his buddy was having his usual pre-church oatmeal and coffee.

Heads swiveled as he burst in and made a beeline straight for the counter where, as predicted, Jeremy sat with a coffee mug poised to his lips.

Seeing Joe, concern clouded his face. "What's wrong?"

"Carrie's gone."

"What do you mean?" He lowered the mug.

"Her car's disappeared."

Kicking into sheriff mode, Jeremy wasted no time getting to his feet. "Think she's headed to Seattle?"

"That's my best guess."

Millie approached them on the other side of the counter, a coffee pot in her hand and a crease in her brow. "Johnny and I saw her driving west out of town on our way in to work. That would be, what, about forty-five minutes ago."

Jeremy tossed some cash on the counter. "Was she alone?"

"Yes." Apprehension etched a furrow in her brow. "Is everything okay?"

Jeremy frowned. "Just give me a call if you see her again."

Joe exchanged a look of apprehension with Jeremy. Without another word, they headed for the door.

Chapter 26

After buying the burner phone and using the antiquated payphone outside the truck stop to activate it, Carrie now sat in her car, digging in her purse for the number Lucas had given her.

Finding a quarter at the bottom, she mentally added it to her tally. The phone had eaten up half her cash, and the full tank of gas Hal had left her with would only get her just so far. Since she'd left before Joe had paid her, she'd have to be careful about what she spent.

Of course, now that she thought about it, she hadn't put in enough time to even pay back what Joe had fronted her for the clothes and car repair, much less come out ahead. Not to mention all the meals they'd provided her with. Once things got back to normal, she'd have to figure out how to send some money to him so they could at least call it even.

She swallowed against a lump that felt like a lead weight. Joe and his grandmother had been so kind to her. And she hadn't even trusted them enough to let them know she was leaving.

She was the worst.

Still searching for the slip of paper, she took a bite of an energy bar and washed it down with a swig of bitter lukewarm coffee from a to-go cup. It wasn't much, but it would have to hold her until she got to Lucas. Of course, she still didn't know where he was.

Hopefully, that would change in the next few minutes.

She found the number and tapped it into the phone, then set the paper next to the energy bar wrapper on the passenger seat, making a mental note to toss it once she felt confident that she'd committed it to memory.

She held her breath till the ringing stopped.

"Hello . . .?"

Her breath hitched at the unexpected sound of a female voice on the other end.

"Is Lucas there?"

A slight exhale. Then, "Who's this?"

"I'm his sister. Who are . . .?" She left her question unfinished as the woman held the phone away from her mouth and spoke indiscernibly to someone in the room with her.

A moment later, "Carrie?" The sweet voice of her baby brother put her heart at ease. "That you?"

"I'm here." She almost cried at the emotion and fatigue straining his voice. "On a disposable, like you said."

"Are you someplace safe?" His voice was so low, she had to strain to hear him.

She glanced at the semitruck she'd parked by to shield her from view of the highway. "Yes. I think so."

"Good."

Muted noises indicated that he was moving to a more private location. Who was he with, and why didn't he want her to overhear his end of the conversation?

Something sounded like a door shutting, then his volume normalized. "Have you seen anything strange?"

"Strange how?"

He let out a quivery breath. "Like someone following you."

She hesitated, the truth hanging back like a dog afraid to leave its kennel. "No." She winced at the lie.

"Okay. That's good. That's good."

"Lucas, you're scaring me. Tell me what this is all about."

He let out a groan, probably hoping she wouldn't ask again. "Okay. Here it is. A guy I know from work, Mac, had some high-end video equipment that got stolen and he wanted my buddy Zander and me to help him get it back."

"Oh, Lucas . . ."

"No, I mean he made it sound like it was no big deal. He'd pay each of us a hundred bucks to go with him to this guy Bill's house with a cop friend of his who was going to be off-duty. The cop was supposed to tell the guy that they knew he had the stuff but that if he let us take it, Mac wouldn't press charges."

Carrie felt like screaming. Why hadn't he run this by her before getting himself into this mess? "That didn't sound suspicious to you?"

"Not really. I mean, Zander was cool with it, so I figured a hundred bucks is a hundred bucks."

Closing her eyes, she leaned her head against her seat. That was Lucas all over. Naive, easily persuaded, and always sniffing out the easy money.

"Anyway, this guy Bill was trying to sell the stolen stuff, so Mac called him pretending to be an interested buyer. He made an appointment for that Saturday night. A week ago. His cop friend picked us all up in this big black SUV. The cop was driving, then there was Mac and Zander. With so many of us, I figured we'd be in and out in a few minutes.

"But the cop just keeps driving till we're out in the boonies. It was totally dark. All I could see outside the car were trees and this big full moon. I started to get the creeps."

Carrie suppressed a shudder at the image.

"It was about then I started thinking maybe this wasn't such a great idea. So I took my phone out and pretended I was reading messages or something. But actually, I opened my audio app and hit Record."

"Oh . . . so that's—"

"What's on my phone. Yeah. Mac and his cop friend started to get more comfortable, and the whole story came out like they thought it was funny. Only it wasn't funny."

Gritting her teeth, she resisted the urge to yell. "I'm going to guess that the stuff wasn't really stolen."

"No, it was stolen all right. But it was stolen from a storage unit where Mac was hiding it to keep it from getting seized as part of a civil suit he lost because he had borrowed money from Bill to start his business and never paid it back."

"So it actually belonged to Bill."

"Right. In a roundabout way. Of course, Mac didn't see it that way. He just kept saying, 'It's my stuff. I have a right to get my stuff back.'"

"And you got all this recorded?"

"Every word." He gulped. "But there's more. We get to the house and Mac tells Zander and me that our job is to look tough and not let the guy get away if he tries to run. Mac pounds on the door and then the cop pulls out a gun."

A gun? Carrie slumped over the wheel, sickened by her hunch about where this was probably headed.

"When Bill opens the door, the cop just bursts in like it's a raid. Then the next thing I know, Mac has a gun too and he's yelling at Bill to put his hands against the wall and at Zander and me to start grabbing the equipment. But when we go to do it, suddenly Bill pulls a gun on *us*. There's this loud noise and a flash and then I realize that there's blood everywhere and Bill is on the floor. Not moving."

Helplessly raising her hand to her cheek, Carrie sat there feeling dazed and a little queasy. This was worse than she'd expected.

"So Zander and me, we just put our heads down and hauled the equipment. Then we all got back in the car and drove to some warehouse. I don't even know where we unloaded it. Mac gave us the cash and we agreed that none of us would admit to being there that night. Then he tells us that if we say anything about what we saw, we're as good as dead."

"Oh, Lucas."

"Yeah, yeah, I know. I'm an idiot." The self-recrimination in his voice was genuine, and sadly, not unfamiliar. When would he actually learn?

"So the next day at work, I tell Zander about the recording. I figure we're both in the same boat, right? And he says we can't take it to the police, because of the one guy being a cop. The police won't help us. We have to just forget we saw anything."

That thought sank into her stomach like a rock. There had to be someone . . .

"But then the police question Zander, and he gets nervous and tells them he can get them evidence in exchange for immunity for both him and me."

"Okay. That makes sense. You weren't part of the planning and neither of you knew there would be guns, right?"

"Except that telling the cops meant telling that bad cop. The one who was there that night. We wanted to turn over my phone, but we didn't know who we could trust. They might just destroy the evidence and maybe frame us. I didn't know what to do. So that was when I brought the phone to you, thinking you could just keep it safe till we figured it out."

"You're a dope." As much as she loved him, she wanted to wring his neck. "Didn't you think about how you were putting my life in danger too?"

"I *didn't* think. You're just always the one I turn to when I need stuff."

Her heart ached. Why was the "stuff" he needed always disaster clean-up and not the good advice that would have prevented the disaster in the first place?

"Anyway," he went on, "the police questioned me and I told them I didn't know anything."

"You lied to the police?"

"I didn't know who I could trust. But I guess the bad cop found out about the recording because he had me followed. That's how they figured I had given my phone to you. And they searched your place. That's when I told you to run. And I ran too."

"And you don't think they're still following you?"

"I've been real careful." A little catch in his voice counteracted the reassuring words.

"Where are you now?" A tear ran down her cheek, and she brushed it away.

"All I could think of was this woman I met when I worked that sales job in Idaho. Her name's Lori."

Great. So her lunkhead brother was on the run from the law, hiding out in rural Idaho at the home of some woman he barely knew. Wouldn't Mom and Dad be proud.

There was no time to waste in reprimands. She had to fix this. "Tell me the address. I can be there in—"

"No." The word was as sharp as a knife. "We should stay separate."

"What? Why?"

"What if they're watching me and you show up? Then they'd have us both."

"Oh, so now you're thinking about my safety? How thoughtful." She drew in a long breath, resisting the accusation that his actual concern was that she might lead them to him, not the other way around. Self-preservation had always been his chief motivator.

"So." She softened her tone. It would do neither of them any good for her to be mad at him. She'd save that for later. "Where does this leave us?"

"We just stay out of sight until the case gets closed."

"Closed? A man died. You think the case is just going to close?"

"Carrie, you have no idea the lengths the cops will go to, to cover up something that one of them is involved in. Yeah, it's going to get taken care of."

She shook her head. As much as she hoped he was right, the idea that anyone would actually get away with murder chilled her to her core.

"But hang on to my phone, just in case we need it."

"I will. It's in my purse."

"Your *purse?* You think that's safe?"

"I haven't exactly had time to get a safe deposit box, Einstein."

"Okay, okay." He lowered his voice, drawing out his words like suddenly he was the consoler. "Don't worry, Carrie Mama Beary. This will blow over and everything will be okay."

The use of his nickname for her felt calculated, but she let it go. She wanted to believe him. What other choice did she have? But as she said goodbye and put the phone away, her own reality clobbered her over the head. She was back to where she'd been a week ago. Nowhere to go. No one to turn to.

Unless . . .

She fingered the phone. She *had* told Lucas's boss she'd let him know when she located him.

One quick, and not exactly cheap, call to directory assistance later, and she was connected with the Absolute Power voicemail. She left Bob a message, letting him know that Lucas was in fact hiding out in Burton. Maybe he could help somehow.

She heaved a sigh. One step at a time.

To be practical, the next step should lead to the truck stop restroom. Wherever she decided to go, it would likely be a stretch between areas of civilization, and the very idea of stopping at an isolated rest area convinced her to toss the rest of her coffee in the trash.

A few minutes later, she emerged from the restroom, feeling no better about her immediate future.

She headed for the glass doors leading outside, and froze. An old red coupe that looked like it might have been used as a stunt car on *Starsky and Hutch* sat behind her Lexus at a weird angle. Her heart drummed as she took another step, straining to see what was going on.

A man materialized from behind her car. His gaze darted around the lot, searching.

For her.

Chapter 27

The back tires of Jeremy's cruiser spit gravel as he pulled out of the parking space, then headed up the main road of town. "Millie says they saw her less than an hour ago. That match up with when you noticed her car missing?"

"Yeah. It was still there last night when Valerie left. That was after one—"

"Hang on." An eyebrow raised, along with one corner of his mouth. "Valerie stayed for another hour after I left?"

"It's not what you're thinking."

"What am I thinking? That she finally nailed your hide to the wall?"

"Yeah, okay. Maybe it *is* what you're thinking." Joe rubbed his eyes. He felt like jumping out of his skin. "Anyhow, I noticed the car was gone sometime around seven."

"Maybe she just went for a Sunday drive." Jeremy picked up speed as they left town and the street became the highway. "You check if her stuff was gone?"

"She doesn't have much 'stuff.' And I told you how upset she was last night. Grandma's skipping church in case she comes back." He cringed inwardly at the thought of leaving Grandma home alone. But, aside from her being down to one arm, this wasn't any different from all the other times he'd had to leave. She'd be fine.

Recouping his professionalism, Jeremy frowned. "How much do you know about her brother?"

"Not a whole lot." Why hadn't he asked? "Name's Lucas."

"Same last name?"

"Far as I know."

Working his jaw, Jeremy reached for his radio.

"Whoa." Joe held up a hand to stop him. "What are you doing?"

"Seeing what Louise can find on him." He paused, not yet pushing the button that would connect him to his weekend desk clerk. "And putting out an APB on Carrie's plates."

"You think that's a good idea?"

"I do if you want to find her."

"But what if there really is some corrupt officer leaking information? Wouldn't we be putting her in more danger?"

"It's a long way from here to Seattle." Letting out a weary sigh, Jeremy seemed to consider. "If you think we're going to find her on our own, you better do some praying."

"I have been."

"Then pray for protection and let me do what I need to do."

Joe weighed their options, then answered with a small nod. "You're right."

He stared out the window, having another little talk with the Lord as Jeremy made the call.

"I hate to say it—" Jeremy gave him a sideways glance. "—but we might not be making things any worse than they are already."

"What are you talking about?"

"I'm thinking about that phone. The one her brother gave her. She use it at all?"

"Couldn't. She didn't know the password. Why?"

He tipped a one-shoulder shrug. "If what she says is true, the guy who's after her might be able to figure out where she is by tracking that device. Even if she just had the thing turned on but didn't use it."

"People can actually do that?"

"People in law enforcement can. So if the guy really does have a friend on the inside—"

"She might not be as well-hidden as she thinks." Joe clenched his hands into tight fists. "We have to find her."

Terrified, Carrie ducked into the convenience store side of the building, stooping low enough to be concealed behind a display of chips. The bell over the door clanged. She peered through a tiny gap between the shelving units.

The man stood in the open space between the entrance to the café dining area and the front counter. With feet firmly planted like a bear ready to attack, his eyes darted around in search of his prey.

"Can I help you, sir?" The counter girl frowned, like she wasn't used to people just bursting in like that.

Ignoring her, he moved to get a better view of the café.

The second he turned, Carrie's breath left her. On the side of his neck was a large bandage.

Like he'd been stabbed.

Clutching her purse to her abdomen, she crept to the far end of the aisle. Maybe he'd go into the café and she could make a run for it.

But instead, he whirled around and started toward her hiding place.

Adrenaline surged. She darted to the back of the store, just in time to evade his detection.

What should she do? Bolt to the front door? He wouldn't do anything to her in front of witnesses.

Or would he?

Panic gripped her. These people Lucas had gotten involved with were crazy.

She scanned the immediate area in search of options. There! Just past a small dairy case, was a pair of aluminum swinging doors. She scurried like a rat, hearing him mutter curse words as he made his way down the next aisle over.

She pushed through the doors into a stockroom where, just past a stack of boxes, she could see sunlight. A back door!

She made a run for it. Shoved the door open. All she had to do was make it to her car.

Rounding the corner of the building, she set her sights up ahead. Her hope sank. A Volkswagen had parked next to her car, pinning it between the semi, the coupe, and what looked like a deep gully. But it was still her only hope for escape.

A horn blared and she stumbled back, realizing that she'd been about to run into the path of a looming semitruck.

Cautioning a look over her shoulder, she saw the man fly around the corner of the building. She darted behind the still-moving truck, and with everything in her, ran for her life.

Thanking God for the auto-unlock on her key fob, she grabbed the handle of the driver side door. But when she pulled, nothing happened. The lock hadn't disengaged.

She looked over the top of her car and saw the man weave around his coupe. Almost to her.

Frantic, she pulled the handle again. "Come on!"

Click. The lock released.

She yanked the door open and dove in, then pushed the Start button. The engine came to life, and she shifted into Drive. But when she reached to close the door, a rough hand grabbed her arm.

She wailed. He pulled at her, but she gripped the wheel and looked ahead at the swampy ravine in front of her. And past that—the highway.

There was no choice. Bracing herself, she ducked down to protect her face.

And gunned it.

He held tight, spewing curse words like fire. The car jolted downward. His grip released. Then the car slowed, but kept moving.

Carrie raised her head, seeing only blue sky for a moment as she traveled up the far end of the gully. Then the highway appeared ahead of her. She finally breathed.

She'd made it.

Shaking so much she could barely pull her door shut, she cautioned a look into the rearview mirror. He was on the ground.

But he was getting up.

Joe had probably never prayed so hard in his life.

Still, with each passing mile marker, a little bit of hope slipped away. How on earth did he expect to find Carrie when they had no clue where her brother might be. Or if that was even her destination.

After riding in silence for several long minutes, Joe was jolted out of his thoughts at the sound of Louise's voice on the police radio.

"Jeremy, code two."

Jeremy grunted, then grabbed the mic. "Louise, it's Sunday. I'm off-duty. That's why I have a deputy."

"Your deputy is ten miles south right now handling another complaint about Sal Andrew's cow getting through the fence and grazing in Tom

Cooper's pasture. This is Rockford, Jeremy. Crime doesn't take a day of rest."

Jeremy sighed. "Code two, go ahead."

"I just got a call about a suspicious person at Wheeler's Truck Stop. You still headed in that direction?"

"Affirmative. Go ahead." He sent an apologetic look Joe's way.

"The counter girl reports that a man entered the premises in a suspicious manner and ran out the back."

"That's it? Go ahead."

"She's afraid he'll come back." She made a *tsking* sound. "It's little Moriah Connor, Jeremy. Kyle's girl. He'd want you to put her mind at ease."

Joe shook his head. While Louise wasn't quite old enough to be Jeremy's mother, she didn't mind exercising a degree of parental authority over him, despite the fact that he signed her paychecks.

"Copy that. I'm en route." Replacing the mic, Jeremy jutted out his jaw. "This won't take long. Police business."

"Yeah." Gritting his teeth, Joe looked out the window. "Police business."

Chapter 28

For the dozenth time, Carrie checked her rearview mirror. Only now, to her horror, a speck of red appeared on the horizon.

She sped up. Checked the mirror again. The speck of red had materialized into the coupe. And it was gaining on her with alarming speed.

"No. No. No!"

Leaning forward as if that might urge her car to go faster, she chastised herself for failing to check a map for outposts of civilization. If she could just stay in the lead till she got to the next town, she could stop and—

Her frantic plan was cut short by a popping sound. She gasped. The coupe was barreling up on her.

Her car lurched. *Oh no.* Had he actually shot her tire?

The *thunk thunk thump* coming from her rear driver side confirmed her horrifying suspicion, but there was nothing she could do. She had to keep going. Her eyes darted from left to right, desperately seeking refuge. Any place where there might be someone who could help her.

Why hadn't she sought sanctuary with the people at the truck stop?

The innocent face of that young girl working the register flashed in front of her. And the people—families and truck drivers—eating breakfast in the café. This lunatic had a gun. If she involved other people, someone else could get hurt.

No. She was on her own.

"God, why?" she bellowed, her voice hoarse with fear. "If You're there, please help me!"

The red car overtook her. Had he just been trying to scare her?

For the briefest moment, she thought her prayer might be answered by his giving up, leaving her behind in the dust.

But in the next terrible instant, he veered in front of her, forcing her to slide out of control. She closed her eyes as her car careened off the pavement and slammed to a stop.

And then . . . silence.

She opened her eyes. Directly in front of her windshield, a tree branch swayed from the impact. Slowly, it dawned on her that she'd swerved off the road and hit a tree. Dazed, she evaluated her situation, but nothing made sense. And why hadn't her air bag been activated?

Then her door swung open and something cold pressed against her temple.

Click.

Instinctively, she raised her hands in front of her. Her heart climbed to her throat, making speech impossible.

When the man spoke, it was low but urgent. "Give me the phone."

She drew in a breath. That voice. She *knew* that voice.

Keeping her head completely still, she shifted her eyes in an attempt to see his face. "Are you . . ." The words rasped like a carrot against a grater. ". . . B-Bob?"

A low chuckle. Oddly devoid of emotion. The gun stayed in position, while he leaned in so close she could smell his breath. *Cloves.*

"You can call me Mac."

Like an arrow aimed at a bullseye, reality struck.

Lucas's boss. His trusted mentor. Bob . . . was Mac. Her attacker. And a cold-blooded killer.

Her head spun and she feared for a moment that she'd pass out. But the prodding of the gun at her head brought her to her senses.

"You're wasting my time." By the feel of the hand he wrapped around her throat, she realized he'd put on gloves. The same ones he'd worn that night in the motel. "Where is it?"

Panicked thoughts flitted through her mind. She had to regain some ground. How many times had she skillfully negotiated a contract for a client? If there was ever a time to put those skills to use . . .

An idea hit and took hold.

"I'll give you the phone." She gulped, hoping he'd loosen his grip on her airway. "But I have a condition."

"Oh yeah?" Removing his hand from her throat, he let out a cackle, like her audacity struck him as hilarious. "This oughta be good."

She swallowed again. "Leave Lucas alone. He didn't do anything."

"Lucas." He straightened, the expression on his face growing dark. "So, that's it, huh?"

He looked out at the rough country surrounding them. A light breeze blew a tuft of hair from his forehead, revealing a receding hairline he'd probably thought it concealed.

"Well, let me tell you something." A corner of his mouth curled as he brought his face down to hers. "It's too late to protect Lucas."

His words echoed in her head, refusing to settle in an order that made sense.

"Wh . . . what do you mean?"

A spark lit in the man's eyes, like he found this enjoyable. "I had him taken care of."

"But . . . that's impossible." The horror of what she thought he was saying was too much for her to accept. "I just talked to him."

"Things happen fast." His mouth flattened into a cruel smile. "After our little conversation the other day, I sent one of my best men out to Burton on a 'job.'" The joviality he injected into that word made her stomach lurch. "He almost gave up. Thought I'd sent him on a wild goose chase. Thanks to your message this morning, he gave it one more shot." He chuckled, like he thought he'd made a joke. "Easier to find something when you're sure it's right under your nose. People in small towns are so friendly and trusting."

In spite of the pressure of the gun, her head snapped in his direction. Burton, Idaho. Where Lucas had gone to stay safe.

And she'd given him away.

Everything in her went numb. Lucas was gone? It couldn't be true. She wouldn't let it be. If she had failed to protect him, nothing else mattered.

"Now . . ." The cold steel traced her jawline, then rested at the base of her neck. "About that deal."

She recoiled in disgust. He could have the cursed phone. She unzipped her purse and reached inside. Her hand brushed against the smooth lining of the pocket, but she felt nothing. She looked down. *Empty.*

Her mind flailed. She'd been so careful. Where was it?

The last time she had it was when she talked to Lucas. She'd been so upset and distracted. Had she absentmindedly stuck it in her pocket? That had to be what . . .

Realization struck. She'd still been wearing Valerie's dress.

"I . . . I don't have it." She closed her eyes, almost hoping he'd shoot her on the spot and get it over with.

"I'm done playing games." Mac reached across her and unfastened her seatbelt. "Get out."

Blindly, she obeyed. It didn't much matter now what happened to her. Keeping her hands raised, she backed up a couple of steps on the uneven ground.

He reached out, keeping the gun leveled at her. "Give me the purse."

She pulled the strap over her head and handed it to him, then watched through bleary eyes as he dumped the contents onto the driver's seat and tossed the bag in the dirt.

When his search proved fruitless, he waved the weapon in her face. "Where is it?"

"I . . . I must have left it somewhere."

"You think you're pretty smart. Hiding from me." He stuck a hand in his shirt pocket and removed a phone, which he tapped at one-handed then put to his ear.

"Yeah, go for it." He spoke forcefully, as if giving a command, then shoved the thing back into his pocket.

Horror filled her. "What did you just do?"

"Shadow Ridge Ranch sounds like a beautiful place."

She stared at him, suddenly alert. "But . . . how did you—"

"Like I said," he sneered, "people in small towns are so friendly and trusting."

"You . . . you went there?"

"Not me. My associate. He's been scoping it out all morning, waiting to see if you were coming back. Too bad you're not there." He pinned her with a steely gaze. "Just the old woman."

A fire of rage flared in her chest, propelling her toward him. "What did he do to her?"

"Careful, now." He shoved her back. "She's fine. Under police protection." His sickening scoff left no doubt in her mind as to what he meant. His dirty-cop friend. "And she'll stay fine. As long as you give me what I came here for."

A renewed sense of urgency surged. "It's at the ranch. But I have a new condition." She raised her chin, wanting to spit in his ugly face. "You can do anything you want to me. Just don't hurt Mrs. Brannon."

He nodded, a repulsive leer creeping onto his face.

Using the gun, he gestured for her to climb the small embankment to where he'd left the coupe. As she did, a premonition struck her to the core.

She'd just signed her own death warrant. And probably worse.

Chapter 29

Joe stared at the rack of magazines next to the front counter of Wheeler's while Jeremy questioned Moriah. There hadn't been much point to waiting in the car, and it felt good to stretch his legs.

"And then, he just ..." She raised both arms above her head, like she was simulating an explosion. "... burst through the doors. Like in a movie or something."

Stifling an eye roll, Joe picked up a copy of *Horse and Rider*. He'd known this girl her whole life, and she'd always tended toward the dramatic.

Jeremy nodded respectfully. "Did he seem like maybe he was high on something?"

Biting her glossy lower lip, she tilted a look upward. "No, I don't ..." Her eyes suddenly widened, flashing back on Jeremy. "Not that I know what that looks like."

"Course not." A little smile raised Jeremy's lips. "What happened next?"

"Well, he just stood there—" Her firm nod indicated the center of the waiting area. "—and looked around. I asked if I could help him, but he totes ignored me."

Tuning out her detailed description of the man's rudeness, Joe glanced up and nodded a greeting to a trucker who had just entered and was veering toward the café. Bored with the magazine, he was about to return it to the rack when a flash of red outside drew his attention.

A sportscar.

Huh. Didn't see many of those around here. Must be either some hotshot kid trying to impress a girl, or an older guy trying to recapture his youth.

"Anything else?" Jeremy's tone now had an impatient edge.

"Oh, yeah. He had this weird thing." Moriah slapped a hand on the side of her neck like she'd just been attacked by a mosquito.

"A thing?"

"Yeah. On his neck. Like, a bandage."

Joe met Jeremy's eyes. By the sudden stiffening of his posture, he knew that his buddy was now taking this girl seriously.

"Did you see anything else? What he was driving? Which direction he went?"

"Um . . ." Pushing a strand of straight brown hair behind her ear, she shook her head. "I didn't really look outside after he ran out the back. I just got my phone and called you."

"You did the right thing." Jeremy reassured her. "Let us know if you see anything else unusual."

She beamed at the acknowledgment of her good judgment.

Following his buddy out the door, Joe felt his sense of urgency rise. Carrie was in big trouble and if he failed to protect her, nothing else mattered.

Carrie squirmed in the driver seat of the coupe, partly because she hadn't moved the seat forward enough, but mostly because of the gun Mac held on her from the passenger side.

Under very different circumstances, this might have been a fun car to drive. It was dinged up on the outside, but the inside at least showed some pride of ownership. Like maybe he was in the process of restoring it, but hadn't gotten to the exterior yet.

On the seat between them, a pack of clove cigarettes explained the smell that permeated the car's interior. And a name tag from Absolute Power Audio Video explained something else. The name on it was Bob McCormack.

Mac.

How could she ever have assumed this guy was trustworthy?

He pinned her with an assessing gaze. "I bet you think you're pretty smart. Tricking me with the wrong phone."

If it hadn't been for the gun, she would have rolled her eyes. "Tricked" him? What, by allowing him to grab her from behind, steal her phone, and then try to kill her? Talk about a skewed perception of reality. She refrained from commenting.

"Then you probably thought you stopped me from coming after you again. Well, that knife of yours is a joke."

Acid surged in her throat. She wanted to point out that her "joke" of a knife had stopped him from suffocating her. But she gritted her teeth and went with a softer tactic.

"It was really smart of you to clean up the room." She released a nervous titter. "You made it look like I was crazy. Like I'd imagined the whole thing."

He snorted. "I figured that would keep the cops off my trail."

"Yeah. It sure did."

"Cleaned up the blood. Cleaned up the pieces of that fake phone too after I smashed it into a million pieces."

Her lips parted but no words formed. He didn't even bother to make sure it was the wrong phone before he destroyed it? And he thought *she* was the dumb one?

Since this guy obviously had an ego the size of Montana, she decided to just keep him talking. "Smart move to slash my tire too."

From the corner of her eye, she saw him give a self-satisfied nod. "Pretty stupid to park back there where no one could see me doing it."

Her heart practically stopped. He was right. Why had she thought that was such a good idea?

"Uh-huh." She needed to keep him feeling in control. "How did you even find me that night? I didn't see anyone following me."

"See, that's where you made your first mistake. Why did you come way out here?" He waved the gun, indicating the sprawling landscape outside the car. "Middle of nowhere."

"I didn't know where else to go."

"Yeah? Well, here's a little hint. You want to stay safe, you stay where there are people. Remember that next time." He chortled at his little joke. "*Next time.* Right."

Her temple throbbed at the not-so-subtle implication. "So you just kept your headlights off? Is that it?"

"Great deduction, Sherlock. You know, I was willing to just let bygones be bygones. If you had given me the right phone in the first place, I would have forgiven you for this little blunder." He flapped a hand at his neck. "And we all could have gone on living happily ever after."

"Wait ..." She frowned, suddenly more curious than concerned about feeding his ego. "You said you destroyed my phone. How did you figure out it was the wrong one?"

"Because, once again, you blew it. If you hadn't turned Lucas's phone on, my buddy the cop wouldn't have been alerted that it was still sending out a signal. He traced it to the nearest cell tower."

Her interest in this conversation vaporized. Lucas had been right. For once in his lunkheaded life, he'd been right.

If only he had warned her sooner.

"Then it was just a matter of checking all the auto repair shops in the vicinity to see who had fixed a tire on a Lexus recently."

She flashed him a glance. He'd called Hal's?

"You know, it can come in real handy to keep cash on hand when you want to get information out of people. My buddy stopped at that auto shop this morning and found a guy who thinks his boss doesn't quite pay him enough. It was real easy to get him to talk about the new girl in town."

Gil? So, the creepy feeling she'd gotten about him had been justified, just premature. Like Joe had said, he was a rat.

So why was *she* the one who'd wound up in the trap?

After alerting the state police to be on the lookout for a suspicious person with the description provided by Moriah, Jeremy had told Joe they'd best continue west on the highway. He'd made it clear that, with so little to go on, it seemed unlikely they'd find Carrie.

But, as far as Joe was concerned, anything was better than sitting still.

Besides, he had to have faith.

Racking his brain for any detail that might be useful, Joe scanned all directions for anything resembling a silver Lexus. "Knowing Hal," he surmised, "he returned her car with a full tank.

Figure she'll have to stop in, what? Four hundred miles?"

Jeremy nodded, distracted.

Joe could tell by the grim look on his friend's face that he wasn't exactly feeling optimistic. He gulped in a breath, refusing to let that discourage him.

As he gazed ahead at the long straight stretch of two-lane highway, something glinted in the sunlight. For a brief moment, he assumed it was a mirage, but when a shape began to sharpen, he leaned forward.

"What's that?" A fresh boost of adrenaline cranked up his pulse. "Looks like maybe a car went off the road."

Jeremy accelerated. "If it's her, my guess is someone *ran* her off the road." The tremble in his voice was subtle but telling.

The closer they got, the clearer the object became.

A silver Lexus.

Jeremy gave Joe a meaningful glance. "Better brace yourself, buddy."

He eased the cruiser onto the shoulder, and Joe was out and halfway down the ditch before he'd even killed the engine. The front of the car was smashed into a tree and the driver door was wide open. And no one was inside.

Even more alarming, her purse and its contents, including her wallet, had been discarded.

Jeremy wasted no time. "Check the immediate vicinity." He charged back to his cruiser. "I'll call for backup."

By the time Joe had circled around and found no indication that Carrie had left the scene on foot,

Jeremy was back and examining the car. The fact that he had donned plastic gloves served as an unwanted reminder that this was a possible crime scene.

Joe stood back, hands on his hips, asking for the Lord's protection over Carrie. Jeremy leaned into the car. When he straightened, he held a small piece of paper in his hand.

"What is it?" Joe took a step closer.

When Jeremy held it out for him to see, his heart climbed to his throat.

A phone number. And a name.

Lucas.

Chapter 30

As the ranch house came into view, Carrie's last hope for escape turned to dust. Mac had told her that, according to the message he'd received from his cop friend, the "old woman" was the only one home. Still, Carrie had held out a hope that Joe would have returned by now and that he would know what to do. But his truck wasn't there.

"Around back."

Gravel crackled like popcorn under the coupe's tires as she drove between the barn and the house. Rounding the corner, Joe's livestock trailer came into view, a bitter reminder of their first encounter. Next to it sat an ominous-looking black SUV.

Her heart broke all over again at the sight of it. If only Lucas hadn't gotten into it last week . . . if he had just walked away from the money . . . none of this would be happening.

"Back door. Move!"

At Mac's prodding, she got out of the car and fell into step in front of him, hands raised like *she* was the criminal here.

Walking as slowly as she could get away with, she regarded the house. If it hadn't been for Lucas's poor judgment, she wouldn't have come here. Wouldn't have brought danger to this wonderful, God-fearing family.

Wouldn't have met Joe.

She trudged up the back steps, a sense of dread enshrouding her.

As she approached the door, she held back. Everything was so quiet. Eerily so. What were they going to find inside? She lingered in this last moment of not knowing.

"Open it," Mac commanded.

She let out a resigned breath, and entered the house.

The smell of bacon and coffee lingered in the kitchen. She hesitated, but the hard, blunt jab to her lower back urged her to continue. Stepping into the corridor that ran alongside the front staircase, she saw that the front doors were open, allowing the cool morning breeze to waft in through the screen doors.

A man in a cop uniform materialized in the doorway to the front room. Though he had a muscular build, he wasn't much taller than Carrie, giving her a fleeting feeling that she was an involuntary extra in a Tom Cruise movie. As they moved closer, she saw to her horror that he also held a gun, which he kept aimed into the front room.

"Good. You're here." He acknowledged Mac with a nod and gave Carrie a quick once-over that made her skin crawl. Then, all business, he disappeared again.

Mac prodded her with the gun, and she followed into the front room.

Relief swelled at the sight of Mrs. Brannon, who sat with her one good hand raised, resting her elbow on the arm of the settee.

Seeing her, the woman broke into a trembly smile. "Carrie!"

Momentarily forgetting the constraints of her captivity, Carrie dashed into the room and leaned down for a quick hug. She whispered in her ear, "Where's Joe?"

"Gone to find you, dear."

"Okay, break it up." Mac yanked her up by the elbow, then held the gun to the side of her head again to drive home his point.

He who holds the gun has the power.

Carrie sent him a scowl, then softened again as she spoke to Mrs. Brannon. "Are you okay?"

"Physically, I'm fine." She shot the cop a pinched look. "This man came to the door looking for you. He says he's a police officer but I don't think he really is."

"He's a police officer, all right." Carrie glared at him as well. "Just not a very good one."

The cop gave her a slow burn. "You'll keep your thoughts to yourself if you know what's good for your friend here."

Mrs. Brannon grimaced. "They say they're looking for your phone. I told them you'd lost your phone, but they don't seem to believe me."

They?

The sound of footsteps coming down the stairs startled Carrie, and she turned her head to see who it was.

A man in his early twenties slowed at the sight of her. An undeniable look of fear flashed across his young features as their eyes locked.

Her breath caught. His athletic build didn't quite go with his baby face, like a puppy who hadn't yet grown into his feet. And something about him seemed familiar. A lost look that only people who've been there themselves can really see. Like someone Lucas would befriend.

"Zander ...?" The word came out so soft, she wasn't even sure she'd said it.

His eyes widened, then he quickly looked away.

The cop snarled at him. "Anything?"

He snapped to attention, then shook his head. "I looked everywhere."

"Doesn't matter." Mac gestured toward the doorway with his gun. "Our tour guide is going to show us all where she put it."

Carrie flung back her shoulders and looked Mac in the eye. "You remember our deal."

"Oh, yes. Gentlemen, the lady and I have agreed that in exchange for the item in question, we will spare Grandma here any harm."

"I beg your pardon." Mrs. Brannon's voice sounded clipped. "But I am certainly not your 'grandma.' My grandson has far better manners. And he's better looking."

Carrie's eyes swelled with tears. Mrs. Brannon was truly the bravest woman she had ever known.

She took in a breath. Might as well get on with this. "It's upstairs."

Leading the way, she felt Mac close on her heels. Peripherally, she saw that the cop had forced Mrs. Brannon to her feet and that they were coming too. Zander brought up the rear.

At the top of the stairs, she noted that all the books in the reading nook had been carelessly tossed to the floor and all the bedroom doors stood open. Anger seethed. She hadn't even considered hiding the phone. This was all so agonizingly unnecessary.

She cautioned a look at Mrs. Brannon, whose face registered pain from either the effort it took to pull herself up the stairs or the sight of her home in such disarray. Probably both.

Their eyes met, and Carrie muttered, "I'm so sorry."

In a show of pure grace, Mrs. Brannon's face softened into a look of maternal nurturing, devoid of all blaming.

Awash in guilt and shame, Carrie started down the hall. But the melodic sound of the doorbell stopped her cold. Everyone in their odd little parade stood stock still, and she looked to Mac for instruction.

Deep furrows creased his brow as he stood there listening. He raised a hand, warning them all to be silent.

Then, a light knock followed by, "Hello . . .. Mrs. Brannon?"

"It's Valerie," Mrs. Brannon spoke softly from where she stood on the top step. "The screen door isn't locked. She'll come in."

At that bit of information, Mac shoved the gun at Carrie's face as he grabbed her arm and forced her back toward the stairs. "Get rid of her." Keeping her close to him like a shield, he maneuvered her down, stopping just above the landing.

His breath felt like hot sludge next to her ear. "You try anything and our deal is null and void."

Terror ripped through her. She had failed Lucas. The same couldn't be true for Mrs. Brannon.

"Now." He pressed the gun to the back of her head as a needless reminder of its presence. "Act normal."

Like a director forcing a reluctant chorus girl onstage, he gave her a little shove. She stumbled onto the landing, into full view of Valerie on the other side of the front door.

Unsuccessfully willing her body to stop shaking, Carrie put on a small smile, as if "acting normal" were even possible under the circumstances. Painfully aware of all that was at stake, she somehow managed to make it down the stairs and across the entryway.

"Morning." Valerie gave her a warm smile.

"H . . . hi." She did her best to keep her voice steady as she opened the screen door. "What can I do for you?"

Valerie took a half step forward, clearly expecting to be invited in, but Carrie blocked her entry. Confusion flitted across Valerie's brow, but she quelled it with another smile.

"I just came to pick up my dress. It's not a big deal, but Mrs. Brannon said she'd bring it to church. I didn't see her there, so I thought I'd save her the trip." She paused, the crease returning to her brow as she flicked a glance over Carrie's shoulder. "She's all right, isn't she?"

Sputtering out a chuckle, Carrie bought herself some time to think of a logical response. "I'm sure she went to church. You must just not have seen her."

"Maybe. But I didn't see Joe either. And they always sit right in front so she can hear the pastor." She flapped her hand, disregarding her obviously justified concern. "It doesn't matter. But if you have the dress, I—"

"Okay." Carrie slipped back inside, allowing the door to shut between them. It was bad enough that she'd brought Mrs. Brannon into this. If Valerie entered the house and somehow got suspicious . . .

Trying to act carefree, she started for the stairs. "I'll just run and get it."

As she rounded the corner of the landing, Mac flashed her a fiery glare. The moment she was out of Valerie's sight, she explained. "She just came to pick up a dress I borrowed. I need to get it."

On the trek to her room, a plan formed. She could smuggle the phone out of the house with Valerie. But what then? What if Valerie found it and came back?

No. She had to get it from the pocket. It was her only bargaining chip.

Stepping into her room, it struck her that nothing really seemed out of place, although Zander had said he'd "looked everywhere." He'd either been less than thorough, or just respectful in his search.

She reached for the dress—which was draped across the foot of the bed where she must have left it in her hurry to get ready to leave—but Mac stepped in front of her.

"Hang on." Keeping his weapon trained on her, he picked up the dress with one hand and shook it. Giving her a suspicious glower, he laid it flat again and shoved his hand into one of the pockets.

Carrie held her breath. If he got the phone, she'd have no leverage. She couldn't let that happen.

She jutted her hand out toward the second pocket, but he got to it first. His fat fist prodded, then came out again. Empty.

As he shoved the dress at her, her thoughts raced. If the phone wasn't in the dress, then where was it?

Folding the dress with jittery hands, she went down the stairs to face Valerie a second time.

"Here you go." Carrie spoke a little too brightly as she opened the screen door and handed over the dress.

"Thanks." Valerie took it, then drew in a breath like she was about to add something. She narrowed her eyes. "You sure everything's okay?"

She wanted to say "no." Give her some sort of cryptic message that things were anything but okay. But she couldn't do it. Not with so much at stake. So she just smiled and nodded as she shut the door, putting the screen barrier between them. "Thanks again for loaning me the dress."

"No problem." Valerie turned and took a step, then paused and faced her again. "And Carrie?"

Carrie swallowed. Waiting. Willing her to just go away before something bad happened.

"I hope you're planning to stay." Valerie smiled sincerely. "Joe really likes you."

Carrie lingered for a moment, torn between the bittersweet message Valerie had just dropped like a bomb, her grief over Lucas, and the pressing matter of Mrs. Brannon's safety.

As soon as the Hayes Family Farm truck started up the drive, she turned to see Mac on the landing.

"She's gone?"

Nodding, she heaved out a breath, pressing a hand to her queasy stomach.

"Good. Now, on with it."

She started toward him, her mind racing to form a new plan to lure the men away from the house, a feat made considerably more difficult now that she didn't actually have the bait to wave in front of them.

At the base of the stairs, she stopped. "Um . . ." *Great start, Carrie. Think of something to say that sounds plausible.* Then a thought struck her. It was worth a shot.

"I forgot. It's not upstairs." She nodded toward the kitchen. "I hid it in the kitchen."

Mac stared at her for a moment through narrow eyes. Then he said something over his shoulder and started down the stairs.

Seeing that they were all trailing along, she headed down the corridor. A desperate plea for this to work looped over in her mind.

Mustering as much confidence as she could manage, she walked into the kitchen and strode over to the counter, then reached behind the cookie jar. Her fingers closed around a solid object.

Yes.

Sending up a prayer that this might at least buy her some time, she faced them, holding Joe's phone like it was the final card in a magic trick.

One corner of Mac's mouth lifted as he reached out and took a step toward her.

"Hang on." She drew back. "What about our deal?"

Mac screwed up his face. "Yeah? What about it?"

"I will hand this over to you once we're all safely away from Mrs. Brannon and this house. That way, I know you're good for your word."

The cop scoffed, then firmed his jaw and let out a little yowl. "You actually think we're going to let an eye witness live?" He shook his head. "Lady, you're an idiot."

He shoved Mrs. Brannon.

As Carrie lurched forward to catch her, she saw the cop raise his gun and take aim at her back.

"Wait!" Her arm shot up to stop him. "You're a cop. If you shoot an innocent person, they'll trace the bullet to your gun."

He lowered the weapon just enough to assure her that he knew she was right. After a long moment, he grabbed Mrs. Brannon by the arm and shoved her toward the open basement door.

Screaming, Carrie dropped the phone and lunged as he hurled the woman down the stairs.

The *thunk* of her friend's landing struck Carrie like a bullet as the cop stepped between her and the doorway.

"You were right." Aiming his gun at her forehead, he forced her to stumble backward.

"Shooting *her* would have been a bad idea. Thanks for pointing that out."

Weeping uncontrollably, Carrie crumpled onto the floor. "You promised!" She wailed, knowing how ridiculous she sounded but not caring.

A vague awareness of the charged conversation between the men fogged her thinking as she closed her eyes and tried to block it out. Mac said something about the phone she'd given them breaking from the impact of her dropping it. Then the talk shifted to making a plan to get out of there and dispose of *her*.

After that, Mac's crass and ugly interpretation of the second part to their so-called deal.

"Consider her your payment." Mac squawked like he thought he was funny. "We'll be waiting outside."

The next thing she knew, she was yanked to her feet. She looked up to see Mac's back as he disappeared into the mud room. Zander cast her an apprehensive look, then headed out the door after him.

Chapter 31

Joe was in serious danger of wearing a trench in the ragged old carpet in Jeremy's office.

Reluctantly, he had allowed Jeremy to talk him into returning to Rockford once the state police had arrived at Carrie's car. They were better equipped to handle that part of the investigation, and Jeremy had wanted to find out if anyone in town had seen anything.

But first, he'd spent the past half hour on his computer trying to get as much information as he could about Lucas.

The phone number they'd found had, so far anyway, been a dead end. Just a *ding*, without an outgoing message to indicate that they had the right number. In the message Jeremy had left, he'd walked the line between scaring the guy off by sounding too official, and being so vague that his motive for calling might be questioned.

Sick of feeling useless, Joe rubbed at a dull ache in his temple. It was about time he checked in with Grandma. But coward that he was, he'd been putting it off in the hope that he'd have some good news to tell her. How was he supposed to break it to her that Carrie might have been taken against her will?

No point in avoiding the inevitable. Besides, he needed to check on Grandma's welfare.

But when he went to get his phone out of his back pocket, he came up short. He patted his shirt pockets too, but still no phone. *Terrific.* Of all the times to remember to bring it with him, this would have been it.

He shook his head. Not that he'd bothered to give his number to Carrie anyway. And if Grandma had needed him, she would have called Jeremy.

No big deal. He'd just borrow the office phone.

As he made his way to the desk, he scanned the computer screen for even the smallest thing he could hang his hope on. "Anything?"

Jeremy shook his head. "This kid has a trail of short-term jobs and old addresses. We can try calling his former employers, but I'm not sure it's going to do us any good."

The ringtone of his cell caused them both to straighten. Reaching for it, Jeremy sent Joe a look that conveyed what they were both hoping for. That Lucas had decided to call him back.

"Sheriff Hingson."

Joe held his breath, waiting for any indication from Jeremy that this might be good news.

As he rose to his feet, Jeremy's expression shifted from serious to urgent.

Using a hold that was probably designed for subduing criminals, the cop had Carrie's arms pinned behind her as he shoved her out of the kitchen. His chest pressed against her back and he poised his gun to her head, a sensation she'd grown surprisingly ambivalent to.

With everything that had happened, she didn't care what became of her. She just wanted it to be over soon.

Despite the despair clawing at her heart, she managed to keep putting one foot in front of the other as he forced her into the front room.

He twisted her arm even harder. "It's up to me to teach you to show respect to those in authority." With that, he released his grip and turned her to face him.

Mustering up every ounce of her remaining energy, she raised her chin and spit in his face. That was all the respect he'd get from her.

Anger flared in his dark eyes as he grabbed her arm. Propelled by a shove, she landed facedown on the settee.

The cop snorted. "You have a lot to learn, lady."

Just as she braced herself for what was to come, a metallic *thwonk* brought a fresh surge of adrenaline. She scrambled onto her side, seeing the cop swagger then, to her alarm, fall to the floor in a heap. Behind him, stood Mrs. Brannon.

"Always use cast iron." Swaying from the exertion, she nodded to the heavy black pan dangling from her one good hand. "You get the best results."

Gasping for breath, Carrie leaped to her feet and charged at her, pulling her into a hug. "You're okay!"

"I told you the doctor taught me a technique for catching myself in case I ever fell again." Her knees seemed to give way and she collapsed into Carrie's arms like a ragdoll. Carrie backed her into a chair and eased her down.

"Thank you, dear." She looked pale, and a little out of breath. "I'm just grateful it's dark down there and they didn't bother to check on me."

Seeing that the experience had taken more of a toll than Mrs. Brannon might be willing to admit, Carrie removed the pan from her quivering hand and set it on the table next to her. "Still, that was an awful fall. Are you hurt?"

"I'll be a little sore tomorrow. But at my age, I'd be sore tomorrow anyway. What's one more complaint?"

She lifted her foot, and Carrie saw that one of her ankles looked like a purple balloon. So much for any plan that involved their running to safety.

The downed officer groaned and both women snapped him a look. While he hadn't moved or opened his eyes, a lump had risen on his temple that rivaled Mrs. Brannon's ankle in Technicolor vividness.

As Carrie studied him for signs of life, a movement outside the front window snagged her attention. She squinted, seeing through the lace curtains that Mac stood on the grass in front of the house, smoking one of his cigarettes. A few yards away, Zander sat on the bottom porch step.

"The other two are waiting outside." Carrie eyed the cop, debating if they could leave him unguarded. "I'm going to the kitchen to call for help."

"I'm afraid we can't use our home phone." Mrs. Brannon *tsked*. "That terrible disgrace to law enforcement pulled the cord out of the wall."

Terrific. And she had broken Joe's phone.

But those weren't their only options.

Biting her lip, she eyed the cop. "He must have one on him."

"He doesn't. He had to use the boy's." With what looked like great effort, Mrs. Brannon raised an arm to point. "But he does have *that*."

Carrie shifted to see the gun holstered between his hip and the floor. Evidently, he'd returned it to his belt in preparation for his lesson on "respect."

Cautiously, Carrie stepped around and stood next to his legs. Considering that some of his weight rested on his weapon, it would be impossible to free it without jostling him. The last thing she wanted was to wake him up. But she had little choice.

Afraid to breathe, she knelt down. What would she do if he regained consciousness and grabbed her before she accomplished her mission? When her fingers grazed the cold surface of the handle, she lost her nerve and drew back.

"You can do it, dear," Mrs. Brannon encouraged. "Have no fear."

She tried again, but it was as if an invisible force field stopped her. "I can't."

"Carrie."

She turned, meeting Mrs. Brannon's warm maternal gaze.

"You *can*." She smiled reassuringly. "Have faith."

Nodding, Carrie flexed her fingers and, with renewed confidence, tried again. This time, she liberated the gun from the holster. Standing quickly, she watched to see if she'd awakened the beast.

When he still didn't move, she shifted her focus to the weighty piece of steel.

She who holds the gun has the power.

"Very good. Now, do what you need to do." Still sitting, Mrs. Brannon lifted the pan from the table where Carrie had set it. "I'll keep an eye on him."

"All right. But if he wakes up, I want you to call for me."

"Yes, yes. Now go."

Unable to stop her limbs from trembling, Carrie crept out into the entryway. Steadying the gun with both hands, she slowly approached the front door.

God, now what?

The question in her own mind took her by surprise. Somehow over the past week, she had gotten back in the habit of turning to God.

But her question to Him remained unanswered. As far as she could tell, Zander was unarmed. But Mac would have no qualms about gunning her down in cold blood. That left her with little choice but to take aim at his back before he realized she was there.

Should she shoot to kill? That didn't seem right. But if push came to shove, this was a matter of survival.

Creeping closer to the door, she peered through the screen and got him in her sights. He still stood there, puffing on his smoke, and gazing impatiently out at the front field.

After reassuring herself that Zander hadn't moved, she edged closer to the door. But something at the top of the steps caught her eye. Mac had left his pack of cigarettes. And something else.

Moving a little closer, she squinted to be sure her eyes weren't deceiving her.

They weren't.

Next to the cigarettes sat Mac's gun.

Relief eased from her lungs. He didn't have his gun. And since she couldn't shoot an unarmed man in the back, this could still end peacefully.

A plan formed. All she needed to do was to get them down on the ground like the cops always did on TV. Then she could grab the other gun and get one of the guys to hand over his phone so she could call for help. It seemed so easy.

And yet, surreally impossible.

She said a prayer, swallowed her trepidation, and pushed her way out the door.

"Hands up in the air. Now!"

Both men reeled around, clearly surprised to see her standing at the top of the steps, arms held straight out with the gun trained on them.

Looking like a scared kid, Zander jumped to his feet, arms raised as instructed. Mac let loose with a scornful laugh.

"Look who thinks she's a Charlie's Angel. Like you'd ever be able to shoot that thing." Still guffawing, he took a step toward her.

She pulled the trigger.

"Aah!" Mac fell to the ground, grabbing his leg. "She shot me!" He fired an accusing glare at her. "You shot me!"

Her heart leaped to her throat as she watched a dark stain spread where he gripped his thigh. She'd actually shot him.

Afraid she might faint, she kept her focus on Zander, who stood there looking up at her and shaking like Jell-O. "Where's your cell phone?"

He flashed a questioning look back at Mac, who was too busy examining his injured leg to notice.

"I . . . don't have one," he stammered.

"Don't lie. I know you do. Just take it out and toss it on the ground."

Flustered now, she tried to recall the order of her plan. She eased closer to the steps, thinking she could use her foot to gently move the other gun behind the column so they wouldn't see what she was doing when she bent to pick it up.

But as she extended her foot, Zander reached around to his back pocket. Alarmed by his sudden movement, she lurched forward, turning her intended gentle tap into a wholehearted kick.

"Hey!"

Mac's shout alerted Zander just as the gun thudded on the ground in front of the porch.

Her eyes met Zander's. In a split second, it became clear that he recognized his opportunity. As he dove for the flower bed, she panicked. She had the upper hand, but only for a moment. It was either shoot him now as he went for the gun, or lose the ground she'd gained.

But she couldn't shoot. He was Lucas's only real friend. Shooting him would have felt like a betrayal of her brother's trust.

Zander scrambled to his feet, holding the weapon in a hand that shook even more than Carrie's. But instead of aiming it at her, he stumbled back, pinching it between two fingers like it was a dead mouse he'd just found.

"Don't stand there like an idiot!" Mac bellowed. "Bring it to me!"

"Don't do it, Zander!" Carrie tried to sound calm but her voice still screeched. "He had Lucas killed. He'll do the same thing to you."

Zander stared at her, eyes widening in alarm. Then he looked away, his face scrunching with emotion. "No . . ."

"You want to go to prison, son?" Mac's voice had taken on that fatherly quality she'd found so endearing back when she knew him as *Bob*. "'Cause that's what's going to happen if we don't take care of this problem *right now*."

"Listen to me, Zander." She somehow managed to approximate the matter-of-fact tone that had won her many a big real estate deal. "There's still time for you to make your plea bargain agreement. You haven't killed anybody. If you participate in killing me, *that's* when you'll go to prison for life."

Zander visibly wavered.

Advancing down one more step, Carrie continued. "People will be heartsick if you let that happen. Who are they, Zander? Your parents? A girlfriend, maybe?"

"I don't have anybody." His shoulders drooped and his voice hitched. "Nobody cares what happens to me. I'm alone."

"No. That's not true. None of us needs to be alone." A knot tightened in her chest. "And you know what? God has something better for you than this."

Surprised by the sincerity behind her own words, she inched a couple of steps closer. She shifted the full weight of the cop gun to one hand and held the other out to him. "Just give me that gun. I'll make sure you get a good lawyer."

He nodded, seeming to take her words to heart.

"You little—" Mac let loose an expletive and lunged in Zander's direction.

Without hesitation, Zander raised the gun and trained it on Mac. His jaw firmed and he glared at him. "I shouldn't have listened to you. You used us. And now Lucas is dead."

As Mac wavered back, a siren wailed in the distance.

Carrie shot up a prayer of thanks.

Chapter 32

As the cruiser careened toward the house, the sight of Carrie and some other guy holding guns on a hunched-over figure both thrilled and terrified Joe. By the look of things, she was safe. But what on earth was going on?

The second the car stopped, Joe was on his feet and sprinting across the yard. Seeing him, Carrie dropped her arms to her sides and started toward him.

Vaguely aware of the deputy's car squealing in behind them and Jeremy taking charge of the situation, Joe took her in his arms. She felt warm and real. And alive. Her body shook as she gave in to sobbing. He tightened his grip, like he might never let go.

But after a long moment, he held her from him, studying her face. "That man. He's the one who attacked you?"

"Y . . . yes."

"Looks like you won round two." He raised a shaky smile. "Are you okay?"

She nodded. "But . . ." Her voice barely registered through the tears. ". . . your grandma is hurt."

Hurt? *No.* "Where is she?"

"Inside." Releasing him, she dipped a nod toward the house. "You should go. I'm fine."

After giving her another assessing once-over, Joe dashed for the house. He took the front steps two at a time and was inside in an instant.

Grandma leaned against the front room doorframe. "Well, praise be."

He hurried to embrace her, slowing only briefly as he noticed the cast iron pan in her hand. Before he could get his arms around her, she lifted the pan in a pointing gesture. He looked into the front room and froze.

"Who's that?"

"One of the bad guys." Her lips went flat with disgust.

"What did you do to him?"

"No worse than he did to me."

He looked down, noting the purple hue to her seriously swollen leg. He was about to ask what had happened when the sound of the front door drew him around. Gun drawn, Jeremy's face registered relief at the sight of Grandma.

Joe nodded into the front room. "There's one more in there, but thanks to David here—" He eased Grandma into the room so he could help her sit. "—I think Goliath will be making his exit on a stretcher."

Jeremy followed them into the room, then trained his gun on the motionless cop. He shook his head, and knelt to check the man's pulse.

"Still breathing." He stood, then muttered under his breath. "Unfortunately."

"Oh, Jeremy." Grandma clucked her tongue. "I know you don't really mean that."

Jeremy shrugged his brows as he removed a pair of cuffs from the man's belt. "Maybe just a little."

Once he had him secured, he kicked the guy's leg, probably not as hard as he would have liked. "Hey, get up."

As the man stirred, Joe heard the screen door open. His heart soared at the sight of Carrie entering the front room.

She threw a disdainful glance at the cop through red puffy eyes. "Jeremy, your deputy said to tell you he's got the other two in the back of his car, and he called for medical assistance."

"I don't need an ambulance." Grandma flapped her one good hand. "I'm fine."

"It's not just for you." Carrie moved to Joe's side, fitting easily under his arm. "It's for the man I kind of shot."

"You did?" Grandma's eyebrows flew up. "Critically?"

She shook her head. "I'm not that good an aim."

A second kick to the man's leg got a groan out of him. "Good, you're awake." Jeremy began reciting his rights, but the man interrupted.

"That woman attacked me." Apparently propelled by anger, he awkwardly pushed himself to a sitting position. "She's the one you should be arresting."

Grandma huffed out indignation. "Don't give him any special treatment just because he's wearing a badge."

"Oh, he'll be getting special treatment all right. *Real* special." Jeremy raised a critical brow. "You can count on it."

While Jeremy finished the process of making the arrest, Carrie elevated Grandma's leg on an ottoman and Joe went to get her some ice. By the time he returned, Jeremy had his prisoner on his feet.

"Young man." Grandma pegged the dirty cop with a stern look. "I don't say this lightly, but I believe there's a special place in hell for any man who intentionally harms a woman. You have a considerable amount of repenting to do if you'd like to avoid going there."

A brief light flashed in the man's eyes before the hardness returned. It was enough to convince Joe that he'd taken the warning to heart.

"Come on." Jeremy prodded him. "You can wait in the back of my car for your medical assistance to arrive. That'll give you plenty of time to regret all your life decisions up until now."

As Jeremy removed him none-too-gently from their house, Joe took a seat next to Carrie on the settee. She looked like she'd been through more than she might care to admit.

"Your grandma said you went out looking for me." She ran her fingers under her eyes. "How did you know to come back here?"

"Well, we found your car, so we figured you were in trouble. Then Valerie called Jeremy. That's how we knew you were here."

"She did?"

"Yeah, she said she stopped by to get her dress and to make sure you were okay." He adjusted the ice bag around grandma's ankle. "She was worried when she didn't see us at church." He directed the next bit at Carrie. "And she said you were acting real strange. Thought Jeremy might want to do a welfare check just to be sure."

Carrie nodded. "Lucky for me, I'm a rotten actress." She smiled wanly, then gave in to tears.

"Hey, hey, hey." He wrapped an arm around her, loving the way she rested her head against his chest.

"I'm sorry." She straightened again. "It's just that, I handled everything all wrong. I failed."

"What do you mean?"

"I was too late to save Lucas." Clutching her stomach, she doubled over in sobs.

Confused, Joe cast a glance at Grandma, who held both hands over her mouth. He turned back to Carrie and placed an arm around her shaking shoulders. "What are you talking about? Lucas is fine."

"No." Sitting up, she shook her head. "That man out there . . . the one who attacked me? He told me that he had Lucas 'taken care of.' I failed him."

"When did he tell you that?"

"A few hours ago."

In spite of her obvious anguish, Joe couldn't help a small smile as he reached into his pocket and retrieved the paper with Lucas's number on it. "Look familiar?"

She frowned. Then as she slowly reached out to take it from him, her eyes regained a measure of hope. "But, how did you . . .?"

"It was in your car. Jeremy left a message and while we were on our way over here, Lucas called us back. Said he wasn't going to but he had a gut feeling he should trust us."

"You . . . you talked to him?" She twisted to face him. "You're sure it was Lucas?"

"Well, he referred to you as his Carrie Mama Beary, so I'm pretty sure it was him."

She spurted out a half laugh. "But . . . I thought Mac had him killed. Why would he say that?"

"He probably thought he had. This morning, some guy tried to break in to the house where Lucas was staying, and the woman he was with freaked out and called the police. They nailed the guy before he could do anything."

"Oh my . . . I need to call him." She looked around. "But I don't have a phone."

"Hang on. I'll go get mine."

He rose from his seat, but she tugged at his arm, forcing him back down.

"You don't have one either. I kind of broke it."

"You broke it. On purpose?"

"I know how much you loved it but no, it was an accident. And the house phone is out of order."

Frowning, he looked between the two women for an explanation.

"It's been quite a day," Grandma said nonchalantly. "We'll have to fill you in."

"So, no house phone. No cell phone. What about Lucas's phone?"

"I have no idea where it is. I thought I accidentally left it behind up in my room, but when I looked for it, it wasn't here."

Grandma raised her hand in exasperation. "Why is everyone so worked up about that thing?"

Joe turned to Grandma, then back to Carrie. "Good question."

"I'll have to fill you in. But that phone is an important piece of evidence. My brother—bless his sweet, stupid, still-beating heart—is going to need it."

"Well, then." Grandma sat up a little straighter. "Let *me* do some filling in."

Joe and Carrie exchanged a look, then turned to Grandma.

She put a hand on Joe's knee. "After you left, I went upstairs to see if you—" She directed that at Carrie. "—had taken your things. I saw Valerie's dress on the bed and remembered that I had told her I'd bring it to her at church. I was going to fold it, but when I found the phone in the pocket, I must have gotten distracted. I was looking at it, wondering whose it was, since I knew you'd lost yours. That was when the doorbell rang, so I put it in my apron pocket and went down to answer."

"So—" Joe gave her a critical look. "—it's in your apron?" Which she clearly was no longer wearing.

"I'm getting to that. It was the police officer at the door. Scared the life out of me at first. I thought for certain that he had bad news. He asked for you, Carrie, but when I told him you weren't here, he got agitated. Then he said he just needed to get your phone and he'd be on his way."

"I'm so sorry I got you involved in this." Joe felt a shudder skitter through Carrie as she said it.

"It's not your fault, dear. I told him you had lost your phone, and that's when he forced his way in. Started looking around. Then he went back to the door and whistled for that young man to come in and search upstairs."

"That must have been terrifying."

"It was more maddening, really. The way they were going through things, I figured it was only a matter of time before they tried to search *me*. It was a good thing I thought of that too, because he made me give him my apron."

"But . . . I don't understand. He didn't find the phone?"

"He didn't find it because it was no longer there. You see, I had figured out that the phone must be the key to what got you in such hot water in the first place. So the instant his back was turned, I put it someplace I knew he wouldn't be clever enough to look." She reached into her sling and produced the device in question.

Carrie let out a gasp. She took the phone, cradling in her hand like it was made of gold. "But they threatened to kill you. Why didn't you hand it over then?"

"I'm no dummy. I knew they wouldn't just leave if they got what they were after. I thought it was worth the risk."

"Oh, Mrs. Brannon. You're my hero."

"Ditto. Now, you should go call your brother." Shifting in her seat, she lifted her good leg to join the other one on the ottoman. "Joseph and I will wait patiently for you to return and fill us both in."

Epilogue

One Year Later

In the softly lit hallway outside their hotel room, Carrie fumbled with her key card. Her hands shook as she waved it in front of the control panel, but nothing happened.

"Need some help with that?" Joe came up behind her, their two suitcases in tow, and placed his hand over hers. Together, they waved the card again. This time, the device beeped and the blue light turned green.

As he lowered the handle and pushed the door open, she gave him a playful smirk. "I warmed it up for you, you know."

"I have no doubt that you're capable of handling things on your own." He kissed the side of her head. "But sometimes it's nice to have someone to lean on."

"I'll give you that." She took a step forward, but he held her back.

"Whoa. Not so fast."

Using his shoulder to prevent the door from shutting, he turned to her. The next thing she knew, he had hoisted her into his arms.

She giggled like a schoolgirl as he swung her into the room. "Well, that was old fashioned."

"You married an old-fashioned guy."

As he set her back on her feet and retrieved their bags from the hallway, Carrie surveyed the room. It was bigger than she'd expected, bright and inviting, with a sliding glass door on the far end that afforded an invigorating view of the Puget Sound.

"Hold on, right there."

He reached through the bathroom door to her left, flicked on the light, and made a show of checking for intruders.

She laughed as he did the same maneuver with the closet, then under the bed. He turned to her. "All clear, ma'am."

"Thank you, sir." Slowly, she crossed the room into his embrace, rewarding him with a long, lingering kiss.

"Come on." Stepping back, she took his hands. "You have to see this view."

With one of his hands still in hers, she led him out onto the balcony and breathed in the salty sea air. Closing her eyes, she rested her arms on the railing and felt the gentle breeze caress her face as Joe eased in behind her and put his arms around her middle.

Sighing, she reached up and ran her fingers across his cheek. While there were things she missed about living in Seattle, she hadn't regretted her decision to relocate to the peacefulness of Rockford. This had been a rough year, what with Lucas and Zander serving time in jail while the terms of their plea deal were negotiated, and Carrie making plans to leave the real estate firm. Now that she had officially moved to Shadow Ridge, her hands would be full helping Mrs. Brannon and learning the duties of a ranch wife.

Wife. She loved how that word resonated in her being.

She leaned back against his chest, enjoying the feeling of his strong arms around her. "Welcome to Seattle, Mr. Moder." She giggled as he kissed her shoulder.

"Thank you, Mrs. Moder." He nuzzled against her hair. "What are you thinking about?"

She held a beat, then said, "About how we're going to divide the closet space in our new room."

He laughed. "We're on our honeymoon, and you're thinking about closet space?"

"You've seen how many pairs of shoes I own."

"Most of which you'll only wear when we come here to visit your brother. I don't know if you've noticed, but high heels aren't a part of our town dress code."

"I'll wear them to church then." She jabbed his ribs with her elbow. "It was nice of your grandma to give us her old room."

"Yeah. I think she was ready to let some things go. It's been good for her."

"Letting go of the past to make room for the future." Carrie gazed out at the sun-dappled water, realizing that the same could be said of her.

She had let go of her old feelings of distrust and disbelief. Traded them for a renewed faith in God and the peace that came with it.

Not to mention, the blessings of being part of a community and a family.

"So . . ." Joe turned her to face him. "What do you do for fun in this town?"

She laughed, melting into his embrace. "You really want to know?"

As their lips met, she reveled in the belief that no matter what, she would never have to feel lost and alone again.

The End

I hope you enjoyed *Benefit of the Doubt*, book 1 in the MONTANA PERIL series.

Please consider posting a review on Amazon or Goodreads. Honest reviews are an encouragement to authors, and help other readers find books to enjoy.

I love hearing from readers! You can find links to my books and contact information at my website:

lesleyannmcdaniel.com

Please enjoy a sample of the next book in
the MONTANA PERIL series.

Hidden from View

MONTANA PERIL ~ Book 2

Lesley Ann McDaniel

Sample

Chapter 1

The bizarre sensation that Janet Locklear had left her body must have been some sort of primal instinct kicking in. How else could she survive this?

Her head felt like a merry-go-round as she homed in on the indistinct voices coming from somewhere in her house. Only two men had been at the door when she'd opened it, right? Why did their urgent conversation sound like a mob?

As she fought back a wave of nausea, she focused on what the men—both deputies if she'd heard them right—said as they walked from room to room, speaking to each other in low voices that echoed in a senseless garble between her ears.

"*. . . no signs of forced entry . . .*"

"... *dust for prints while* you *go around to the back* ..."

This was all happening so fast. And yet time had somehow stood still.

The distinct flash of a set of headlights in her driveway swooped through the front window. Looking up as one of the deputies opened the front door, it struck her how dark it was out there. She had wanted to get away from people, but why hadn't it occurred to her how isolated and vulnerable she'd be in this house? Surrounded for miles by nothing but woods. And the river ...

A fresh wave of queasiness struck at that thought, and the sickening trail it led her down. All of a sudden, her vision faded to black and everything around her began to spin like some crazy carnival ride. Her knees gave way, and she started to go down.

But in the next moment, a pair of strong arms scooped her up then set her carefully on a soft surface. Voices, deep and weighted with concern, came from all around her, but she couldn't quite make sense of what they said. She fought to open her eyes.

When she did, a face, blurry and indistinct, hovered inches over hers.

Kind. Handsome.

And unfamiliar.

Light brown hair and a stubble of beard, suggesting that his sleep had been interrupted by her emergency call. His eyes—deep blue, if she wasn't mistaken—looked at her with intense concern.

"Mrs. Locklear?"

She jolted at the sound of her name. So he knew who she was . . . but who was *he?*

"Mrs. Locklear. I'm Sheriff Hingston. Can I ask you a few questions?"

As she tried to sit up, he placed a supportive hand under her shoulder. Realizing that the surface she'd been placed on was her sofa, she swung her legs to the floor. The sheriff gave her an assessing look as he raised himself from where he'd been kneeling next to her.

"Hey, Bobby." He called out to one of the other men. "Grab her a glass of water, would you?"

"Sure thing, boss."

While the deputy disappeared into her kitchen, Sheriff Hingston took a seat next to her and removed a notepad from his pocket, adding to her sense that this had to be a bad dream riddled with clichés from too many late-night crime dramas.

"I know you've had a lot to deal with, but time is of the essence here." He cleared away the huskiness in his throat. "I'm sure you understand."

Not wanting to think about the deeper meaning of that statement, she simply nodded.

The sheriff acknowledged the deputy as he placed a glass of water on the table next to her. "Now . . ." He reached across her to reposition the glass onto a coaster, then wiped away the ring of moisture it had left behind on her secondhand end table. "Tell me what happened."

Her eyes fixed on the glass and the wet smudge next to it. It struck her that an officer who would pay attention to that kind of detail must be really good at his job.

The thought brought a moment of solace.

She swallowed hard. "Well ..." Licking her parched lips, she pulled together her thoughts. "I woke up and couldn't go back to sleep, so I came out here to read for a while." Absently, she gestured to the book on the coffee table.

"And what time was that?" The pen in his hand clicked. "Do you recall?"

"I don't know. Maybe an hour and a half ago. What time is it now?"

He checked his watch. "Three fifteen. So you woke up at around one forty-five. Does that sound right?"

One shoulder lifted. "I guess." She nodded. "Yes. Now that I think about it, I did look at the clock and it was a little before two."

He jotted something in his notepad. "And what happened next?"

"After a few chapters, I felt tired. I went back down the hall, and ..." Her voice broke and her eyes felt like they might explode. "... and I opened the door to my son's room. To check on him one more time. Just in case ..."

"And what did you see?" The question was soft but pointed.

"Nothing. He was just ..." She gulped, barely able to get a breath strong enough to support her next word. "... *gone.*"

Sample

Chapter 2

If there was one thing Jeremy hated about his job, it was feeling powerless to console a grief-stricken victim. But something about Janet Locklear made him want to try even harder than usual.

In spite of her splotchy face and puffy, reddened eyes, her attractiveness was evident. But that wasn't the reason he felt an extra dose of compassion for her. Her situation brought to mind his own near-tragic past. A past that had shaped his entire life.

As he watched her sip water from the glass Bobby had brought her, Jeremy cleared his throat. "Mrs. Locklear . . . where is your husband?"

Her gaze cut to him, and it seemed that the glass almost slipped from her hand. "He's . . ." She looked away, blinking like the question had struck a fresh nerve. "He died. Three months ago."

He instantly regretted having asked the question. Not because it wasn't necessary, but because it had clearly added to this poor woman's trauma. "I'm so sorry."

She nodded, carefully resetting the glass on the coaster. "Thank you. It was sudden. A plane crash."

"I see." He made a note of that, not wanting to press her for details, particularly when it didn't seem relevant to the case.

While he hadn't actually met her until tonight, he had been aware of someone moving into the old Peterson place. Rockford was a small town and it was part of his job to be aware of who came and went.

She'd moved in a couple of weeks earlier and, if the scuttlebutt at the diner could be believed, had pretty much kept to herself. In fact, except for a reported sighting or two at McNarry's Market, she hadn't shown her face in town. That had seemed unusual, but now that he knew she'd been recently widowed, it made more sense. Grief was often a solitary activity.

He considered what to ask next. "Any other family?"

"My sister. But we aren't on speaking terms."

He noted that too. "And does she live here in Montana?"

"Ohio." Her brow creased. "I'm sorry, but I don't see what that has to do with—"

"We need to cover all our bases. Anyone you can think of who might have a reason to take . . . What's your boy's name?"

"Caleb." The word came out in barely a whisper.

"Caleb. Anyone who might have a reason?"

"Of course not."

He nodded, sensing the clock ticking on her patience. "Any unusual encounters with anyone in town?"

"No. I mean, I haven't left the house much. I work from home. Why?" Her gaze snapped from her lap to his face. "Is there something you're not telling me?"

Her question confused him until he realized how it must have filtered through her terrified mind. "Not at all. Rockford is a very safe town. It's just that, we don't have much to go on here."

She nodded again.

"Any chance he might have wandered off on his own?"

"I don't see how. He's only two. The front door was still bolted when I let the deputies in. But ..." She jarred, like a thought had occurred. "I didn't check the back."

"My men checked. It's still deadbolted as well. And all the windows are locked. I just needed to ask."

"He's never done anything like that. He's just a baby."

"Yes, ma'am."

"Sheriff?"

At the sound of Bobby's voice, Jeremy raised his eyes to where he had appeared at the end of the hallway. A slight motion of his head indicated that he wanted to have a word with him in private.

"Excuse me just a minute."

At her barely perceptible nod, Jeremy stood and directed Bobby into the kitchen.

"What've you found?" Jeremy kept his voice low, not wanting to add to the poor mother's worry unnecessarily.

"Not much of anything. Kyle's taking another look around outside, but until it gets light it's hard to see if there are any footprints."

"Ground's so dry, we might not find any even if someone was out there."

"Right. There's no note. No evidence of foul play."

"No known offenders in the immediate vicinity. But that doesn't rule out the possibility of someone following her here."

"You bringing in the county on this one?"

"Already called them." Jeremy ran a hand across his face. "This is too big for you, me, and Kyle to handle. Especially with nothing to go on."

"So, what happens now?"

He let out a breath. This was by far the biggest case he'd had since taking over as sheriff. He and his men were used to the daily grind of speeding tickets and neighborly spats, but they'd never faced anything this serious. He said a quick prayer that they would be up to the task.

"I'll go into town to help Louise organize the search while we wait for the county officers to show up. They ought to be here by daybreak. In the meantime, I want Kyle to keep watch outside while you secure the boy's bedroom as a possible crime scene."

A soft gasp brought his head around. Janet stood in the doorway looking like she'd just been struck across the face.

Her hand trembled as she clutched the fabric of her robe, pulling it tighter around her neck. "Why are you just standing there?" Coming toward them, she raised her other hand and jabbed a pointed finger in the direction of the window over the sink. "He's out there. My baby is out there. Why aren't you looking for him?"

"Mrs. Locklear. We're doing all we can." Keeping his emotions in check, he gave Bobby a subtle signal to get to work on his appointed task. "We set the wheels in motion for an organized search of the area. We'll issue an Amber Alert. Trust me." He looked into her eyes, hating the fear and anguish he saw in them. "We're doing everything we can."

In spite of his reassurance, her eyes pooled with tears.

"Is there anyone we can call for you?"

"No." She shook her head. "There's no one."

Odd. Did she really mean she had no close friends or family, or just no one she wanted him to call at this hour?

Resisting an urge to put a comforting hand on her shoulder, he closed his notepad and returned it to his pocket. "I'm leaving my two men here while I go into town to get the search started. Do you have a recent picture of Caleb we can use?"

Wordlessly, she stepped over to the refrigerator and removed a photo from under a dinosaur magnet. Running her fingers across her cheek, she glanced at it briefly, then handed it to him. The tiny smiling face looking up from the photo tugged at his heart. She was right. He was just a baby.

Not knowing what else to say, he headed for the door.

"Please."

He turned back, surprised by the feel of her hand on his arm.

Her eyes pleaded with him. "You have to find him."

Stricken by the weight of that responsibility, he made a silent promise with a slight nod, then said a prayer as he headed for the front door.

God, I need You here. Show me what to do.

End of Sample

Newsletter Invitation

My Thank You Gift to You . . .

High and Dry

CRESCENT COVE series Prequel

Available only to my newsletter subscribers. Get your copy for FREE!

Do you love Inspirational Fiction? Join my newsletter family and receive all the latest news about my books, plus contests, giveaways, and insider info.

www.lesleyannmcdaniel.com

ABOUT THE AUTHOR

Born in Missoula, Montana, Lesley earned a degree in acting at Willamette University in Salem, Oregon. She fell in love with theatrical costuming, and pursued that as a career while nurturing her passion for writing on the side.

Between working as a home-schooling mom and a professional theatre costumer, Lesley has completed several novels and screenplays. She would have done more by now if she didn't occasionally stop to clean the house. Fortunately, she loves to cook, so no one in her family has starved yet.

Lesley now resides in the Seattle area with her family, including three cats and a big loud dog. She is a member of the Northwest Christian Writers Association.

Her first movie, *Home Sweet Home*, was released in 2020.

In her spare time (ha!), she chips away at her goal of reading every book ever written.

Please visit her website at:
lesleyannmcdaniel.com

www.ingramcontent.com/pod-product-compliance
Lightning Source LLC
Chambersburg PA
CBHW030113180626
46812CB00002B/399